The]

Brynl House

By

Caroline Clark

Caroline Clark

Introduction

This book is based on a true story about a real haunted house that is situated in Kent, United Kingdom. Called The Cage it is reputed that it once served as a prison and is said to be haunted by the vengeful spirit of a woman, Ursula Kent who was executed for witch craft in the property.

In the 16th century it is said that 13 women accused of being 'witches' were hung there after being subjected to torture.

The property shot to fame in 2012 when then owner Vanessa Mitchell, said she was forced to escape the house when she saw a black shadowy figure standing over her infant son.

Since then the house has developed the reputation of being one of Britain's most haunted. It is currently occupied by Micky Rawlings who is researching a documentary about the supernatural and admits he must be a bit bonkers to live there.

The poltergeist in the property have been accused of scratching, and even biting those who dare to stay there.

"I'm not a religious man and yet I go to bed every night clutching a crucifix for my own safety," Micky said.

"After a few days, I got to learn the natural noises of the house. Now the non-natural noises keep me awake at night."

I hope you enjoy this ghost story based on a real live haunted house. I have moved the location of the house and much of the story is fiction, however there are some bits that are based on the truth and my own interpretation of the truth.

Now you know a little bit about the house, dare you read this chilling tale?

Caroline Clark

TABLE OF CONTENTS

License Notes

This story is a work of fiction any resemblance to people is purely coincidence. All places, names, events, businesses, etc. are used in a fictional manner. All characters are from the imagination of the author.

Prologue

25th April 15 82
The basement of the cage.
Derbyshire.
England.

3:15 am.

    Alden Carter looked down at his shaking hands. The sight of blood curdled his stomach as it dripped onto the floor. For a moment, his resolve failed, he did not recognize the thin, gnarled fingers. Did not recognize the person he had become. How could he do this, how could he treat another human being in this terrible way and yet he knew he must. If he did not, then the consequences for him would be grave. For a second he imagined a young girl with a thin face and a long nose. Her brown hair bounced as she ran in circles and she flashed a smile each time she passed. The memory brought him joy and comfort. Brook was not a pretty girl, but she was his daughter, and he loved her more than he could say. He remembered her joy at the silver cross he gave her. The one that he was given from the Bishop, the one that cost him his soul.

Rubbing his hands through sparse hair, he almost gagged at the feeling of the crusty blood he found there. How many times had he run those blood-soaked fingers through his lank and greasy hair? Too many to count. It had been a long night, and it was not over yet. This must be done, and it was him who had to do it.

Suddenly, his throat was dry, and fatigue weighed him down like the black specter of death he had become. A candle flickered and cast a grotesque shadow across the wall. Outside, the trees shook their skeletal fingers against the brick and wood house and he closed his eyes for a moment. Seeing Brook once more he strengthened his resolve. The trees trembled, and the wind seemed to whisper through their leaves, tormenting him, telling him that he was wrong but he would not stop. Could not stop. Taking a breath, he felt stronger now, and with a shaky hand, he picked up an old stein and took a drink of bitter ale. It did not quench his thirst, but it gave him a little courage. He must do this. He must go back down to the cage and finish what he had started, for if he did not Brook would not survive and maybe neither would he?

The kitchen was sparse and dark and yet he knew he was lucky. The house was made of brick as well as wood. It was three stories' high and was bigger than he needed. This was a luxury few could afford. As was the plentiful supply of food in the pantry and work every day. The Bishop had been kind to him, and he knew he had much to be grateful for. Yet, what price had he paid? As the wind picked up, the trees got angry and seemed to curse him with their branches. Rattling against the walls and making ghostly shadows through the window. Alden turned from them and up to the wall before him. The sight of it almost stopped his heart and yet he knows he must go back down to the cage. If the Bishop found him up here with his job not done, then he would be in trouble... Brook would be in trouble. A shiver ran down his spine as he approached the secret door. Reaching out a shaky hand he touched the wall. It was cold, hard and yet it gave before him. With a push, the catch released and the door swung inward. Before him was a dark empty space. A chasm, an evil pit that he must descend into once more.

Picking up the oil lamp, he approached the stairs and slowly walked down into the dark. The walls were covered in whitewash, and yet they did not seem light. Nothing about this place seemed light. Shadows chased across the ceiling behind him and then raced in front as if eager to reach the hell below. Cobwebs clawed at his face. These did not bother Alden, he did not fear the spider, no, it was the serpent in God's clothing who terrified him.

With each step, the temperature dropped. He had never understood why it was so much colder down here. Cellars were always cool, but this one... with each step, he felt as if he was falling into the lake. That he had broken through the ice and was sinking into the water. Panic clenched his stomach as he wondered if he would drown. The air seemed to stagnate in his lungs, and they ached as he tried to pull in a breath. It was just panic, he shook it off, and was back on the stairs. His feet firm on the stone steps he descended deeper and deeper. He shrugged into his thick, coarse jacket. The material would not protect him, of that he was sure, but he pushed such thoughts to the back of his mind and stepped onto the soft soil of the basement floor.

There was an old wooden table to his right. Quickly, he put the oil lamp on it. Shadows chased across the room. In front of him, his work area was just touched with the light, he knew he must look confident as he approached the woman shackled to the wall. Ursula Kemp was once a beauty. With red hair and deep green eyes. Her smooth ivory skin was traced with freckles, and she had always worn a smile that had the local men bowing to her every need. Seven years ago she had married the blacksmith, and they had a daughter, Rose. Alden felt his eyes pulled to his right... there in the shadows lay a pile of bones. A small pile, the empty eyes of the skull accused him. Though he could not look away from that blackened, burned, mound... the cause of another stain on his soul. Bile rose in his throat, and the air seemed full of smoke. It was just his imagination, he swallowed, choked down a cough and pulled his eyes away. Blinking back tears, he turned and looked up at Ursula. Chained to the wall she should be beaten, broken, and yet there was defiance in her eyes. They were like a cool stream on a hot summer's day. Something about them defied the position she was in. How could she not be beaten? How could she not confess?

"Confess witch," he said the words with more force than he felt. Fear and anger fired his speech and maybe just a little shame. "Confess, and this will be over."

Ursula's eyes stared back at him cool, calm, unmoving. She looked across at the bones, and he expected her to break. Yet her face was calm... her lips twitched into a smile.

Alden's eyes followed hers. The bones were barely visible in the dark, but he could still see them as clear as day. A glint of something sparkled in the lamplight, but he did not see it. All he could see was the bones. Sweat formed on his palms as if his hands remembered putting them there. Remembered how they felt, strangely smooth and powdery beneath his fingers. *Ash is like silk on the fingers...* a sob almost escaped him, and for a second he wanted to free Ursula, to tell her to run... and yet, if he did then the Bishop may turn him and Brook into a heap of ash like the one he was trying to not look at.

In his mind, he heard the sound of a screaming child, the sound of the flames. Smelt the burning, an almost tantalizing scent of roasting meat. Shaking his head, he pushed the thoughts away. Now was the time for strength. Biting down on his lip, he fought back the tears and turned to face her once more.

"You will not break me," she shouted defiantly. "Unlike you, I have done no wrong. Kill me, and I will haunt you and your family until the end of time."

Alden turned as anger overrode his judgment, striding to the table he picked up a knife. It was thin, cruel, and the blade glinted in the lamplight. Controlling the shaking of his hands, he crossed the room and plunged it into her side. For a second it caught... stopped by the thickness of her skin. Controlled by rage, he leaned all his strength against it and it sliced into her. Slick, warm blood poured across his fingers. "Confess, confess NOW," he screamed spraying her face with spittle.

A noise from above set his heart beating at such a rate that he thought she must hear it. It pounded in his chest and reminded him of his favorite horse as it galloped across the fields.

The Bishop was here.

Without a confession, he was damned, but maybe he was damned anyway. Maybe his actions doomed him to never rest, yet he must save his daughter, he must save his darling Brook.

As he heard the door above open, panic filled his mind, he must act now, or it would be too late. Then he saw it in her eyes, Ursula knew what was coming. She knew she would die soon and yet she did not fear it. Maybe she thought she would meet her daughter, that they would be together again. He did not know, but the calm serenity in her eyes chilled him to the bone.

In a fit of rage, he struck her on the temple. The light left her eyes, her head dropped forward, and she was unconscious, but it no longer mattered... he had a plan.

"You have confessed," he shouted. "You are a witch. By the power of the church, I sentence you to death, you will be hung by the neck until you die."

Before the Bishop reached him, he pulled back his hand and slapped her hard across the face. The slap did not wake her, but the noise resounded across the cellar. As the Bishop stopped behind him, he felt an even deeper chill. This man had no morals, no conscience. Alden knew what he had done was wrong, but he did not care. If it kept his family safe, he would sacrifice any number of innocents, and yet his stomach turned at the thought of what was to come.

"You have your confession," the Bishop's voice was harsh in the darkness. "Let us hang her and end this terrible business."

***

Ursula woke to the feel of rough, coarse hemp around her neck. As her eyes came open, she felt the pain in her side and knew it was a mortal wound. The agony of it masked the multiple injuries she had received over the past few days.

Alden was holding her. Hoisting her up onto a platform which was suspended over the rail of the balcony. The rope tightened as he placed her feet on the smooth wood and fear filled her. This was it, she knew what was coming, and yet she shook the fear away. To her side, the Bishop stood, a lace handkerchief in his hand as he dabbed at the powder on his face. Blond hair covered a plump but handsome visage, with good bones and a wide mouth, but his eyes... they were gray and hard. The color of a gravestone they could cut through granite with just a look. Amusement danced in them, or maybe it was just the lamp flickering. It could not provide nearly enough for her to really tell, and yet she knew.

Alden moved away from her and turned to the Bishop. There was a hardness to him too. His lips were drawn tight enough to make a thin line, but he could not fool her. Alden was afraid, and she pitied him, pitied the days to come. For her, it was over. Death would be a sweet release, but for Alden, it had only just begun. As he pushed the table, she looked down to the floor below. The lamp did not light more than half way, and it seemed that she would jump into a bottomless pit. If the rope did not stop her... then maybe she could fly. Down deep she hoped she would soar, away from pain, away from fear and safe in the knowledge she held.

If only.

The moon came from behind a cloud and shone through the window at her back. Its light cast shadows through the branches of a large, old oak tree. Sketchy fingers coalesced on the far wall, and her heart pounded in her chest.

Was this a sign?

A welcome?

The shadows danced and then formed and appeared to be a finger pointing to her doom.

It was time.

Before Alden could push her, she stepped out into nothing.

Chapter One

1st March 2017
New Hope Women's Shelter,
105 Baxter Road,
London.
England.
11.30 am.

Emma Kemp stared down at two folded letters on her lap. The paper was not only different but at the complete opposite ends of the spectrum. The one on the left was a warm butter color, thick, heavy, and expensive. Lynn had told her it was laid paper, old fashioned and favored by top end solicitors. To prove the point the top was monogrammed in gold letters.

Harvey, Bentley, and Partners.

Solicitors at Law.

It offered a future, a new beginning, but just looking at it made her stomach roll.

In her right hand was a folded piece of printer paper, 80 gsm. It was delivered by the box load on a monthly basis and was the cheapest one they could get their hands on. Emma remembered the last delivery and her fear at signing in the box. It meant getting close to the delivery driver, and that was something she could not do... not yet... and especially not now. Not when she had known that this letter was coming. Instinctively her hand went to her right shoulder. The break was healed now, but sometimes it still ached.

A tear dropped from her eye, and she wiped it away, angry that she was letting her feelings show.

A knock at the door caused her to jump and set her heart beating faster. Jerked to her feet, she tossed the letters on the small white dresser. It felt good to let them go as if that would make it better.

A mirror above stared back at her. Quickly, she ran a hand through her long brown hair and flicked it over her shoulders. Big brown eyes were lined red from her tears, but there was nothing she could do about that now.

"Come in," she called and was pleased her voice did not shake. After all, this time came to them all, why did she think it would be different for her?

"Hi, Emma," Lynn almost bounced into the room. Her ash blonde hair was tied in a low ponytail, and as always her face bore a smile. "You missed breakfast, everything all right?"

Emma's big brown eyes flicked across the small and spartan room to the dresser and the two letters there. A lump formed in her throat and she had to bite back more tears.

Lynn sat on the bed and taking Emma's hand she pulled her down next to her. The cover was cotton and crisp and the bed firm. This small room had been her home for almost a year, and Emma could not face a future without it. Without Lynn and the other women. They had become her friends, her family, and her security blanket, she did not want to leave. A hand touched her shoulder, and she jumped. With heat spotting her cheeks she turned to Lynn and shrugged an apology. "I... I feel so lost."

Lynn turned to face her, and there was understanding in her eyes. "I know," she said.

Those two words were so good to hear. Emma was feeling guilty. She had been at the shelter a year, and if she stayed, it meant another woman could not take her place, could not find safety and the healing power of Lynn

Chambers and the wonderful women who helped her. After her injuries and mental scars had started to heal, Emma had been one of those women, and she had hoped that she could stay on and work there permanently. The problem was there was no position, or at least no money to pay her, and plenty more volunteers to take her place. It was time for her to go but she just didn't know if she had the courage.

"You have been so good to us here," Lynn said. "We will all miss you, but you need to leave. Not for us but for yourself."

Emma turned to her friend. At 36 Lynn was ten years her senior and yet they had hit it off from day one. When Mark had finally put her in the hospital, Emma had felt as if her life was over. How would she escape him? How had she let this happen and what would she do next? Lying in the bed, battered and broken, she did not know where to turn. When Lynn had bounced into her room, all smiles and positive energy it had seemed like a dream. Yet, before she knew it, she was living in New Hope Women's Shelter. Mark had no way of finding her, and she was starting to heal.

"I don't want to leave," she said the words before she realized and gave Lynn a look of shame.

Her friend pulled her into her arms and held her tight. "I don't want you to go, but I know it will be the best thing for you. Now tell me all about this house."

Emma reached for the solicitor's letter and told her again about the relative she never knew she had, and the mysterious house she had been left in Derbyshire. She knew this was a technique to get her used to the idea. She had done the same thing with new women in the shelter. Just let them keep telling the tale until it becomes familiar and therefore less scary.

"Do you really think it is right for me to leave?" she asked.

Lynn nodded. "You will never fully recover if you stay here... and you know it."

***

It was just two weeks later that Emma was finally ready to leave. She had been called to the lounge and was grinning as she came around the door. Though they thought they were being sneaky, she knew what to expect. As she walked into the lounge a cacophony of cheers greeted her. Soon she was engulfed in twenty sets of arms as the women hugged her so tightly she thought she might break.

Following copious amounts of cake, tears, and some laughter Lynn had helped her to her car. It was an old and battered Volvo x60. The gold paint was chipped in places, and the rust showed through on the wings, but it was hers, and she was proud of it. It seemed strange after her reluctance, but now that she was ready to leave Emma was looking forward to the future.

Lynn placed a parcel of wrapped cake on the passenger seat and came around to take her hands. Emma squeezed gently and smiled. Then she was engulfed in Lynn's arms and hugging her close.

"I will miss you," Lynn said. "You are special... I know I should not say it, but I really feel that we are good friends."

Emma nodded, blinking back her tears and trying to swallow the lump in her throat.

"You call me any time of the day or night," Lynn said as she pulled back.

Emma nodded.

"I will, but I will be all right... thanks to you I will be all right."

***

After three and a half hours in the car, Emma pulled up outside her new house. The last thirty minutes had been fraught and difficult, and she had gotten lost twice. As the sun began to set she had taken a wrong turn, being sure that she must be here already, but no, the sat nav had just taken her further and further away from the pretty little town of Castleton. The roads were narrow and lined with trees and by the time she pulled onto the lane that led to the house she was tired, hungry, and just a little scared.

Turning off the engine, she peaked through the trees at her new home. It was a big house of three stories and was surrounded by tall trees. There was something a little lost and neglected about the place, and for a moment she shuddered.

What was she, a city girl, doing here?

Her hand reached down to the keys. Maybe she should just go back. Then she thought of the drive, and she saw Mark's face. The way his eyebrows knitted together when he was angry. The red that scoured his cheeks and then the thinness of his lips that always proceeded the pounding of his fists.

The old fear came back, despite Lynn and the shelter's best efforts. Yet she knew her friend was right. It was time to get out into the world. Though she knew she would never trust a man again, at least she could live an independent life.

Quickly, she pushed all thoughts of running back to London to the back of her mind. No, she was here, and it was a new start. "Thanks, Aunty Kemp," she said as she found her phone and quickly typed a text to let Lynn know she had arrived safely. As she sent the text, the phone flashed at her. No Signal.

"Damn." That was a good start.

She opened the door and picked up her

bag. On top of it, she placed the cake. It wasn't the healthiest of meals, but it would do for tonight.

Getting out of the car, she found her legs a little rubbery. Concerned, she searched the trees for the solicitor who was supposed to meet her. A Mr. Harvey.

The walk up to the house seemed a long way. There was a concrete path, but it was dark and a little slippery. Something spongy gave beneath her feet with each step. *Moss!*

Emma stepped beneath the trees and the shadows darkened. The leaves seemed to whisper above her, like silent conspirators. Urging her on or urging her back, she did not know.

As she stepped from the trees, she saw her house fully for the first time, and she was a little disappointed. It was old, a little weary looking and yet it had once been grand and proud. The windows were dark and ominous, and on the front, a name plaque seemed to be slipping off the wall.

Brynlee House.

There was no sign of Mr. Harvey but on the door was taped an envelope. Emma quickly opened it and feeling the wind chill around her neck, she shivered slightly. Inside was a key and a short note explaining where the light switch was, that the power was sometimes intermittent and that the phone would be on in a few days. At the bottom was a number for her to contact him in case of emergency.

In case of emergency?

Emma stared at the key. It was large and old-fashioned and felt heavy in her hand. Once again the urge to leave came upon her. What was she doing here?

Taking a breath, she put down her bag, put

the key in the lock and turned it slowly. She pushed the door open. Behind her the trees murmured louder, it felt a little like approval, and she stepped into her new home.

It was easy to find the light switch. A dull yellow light lit up a large entrance hall. It was dark and dreary and like something from a different century. Directly in front of her was a curved staircase and behind that, a window. The moon shone through, and tree branches danced in their light. As she picked up her bag, the door slammed behind her, and the lights went out.

Caroline Clark

Chapter Two

Emma froze in the darkness as fear clenched onto her heart. A scream formed in her throat but she bit it back. All around her, the trees whispered, murmured, and seemed to mock her fear. Emma dropped her bag and scrambled in her pocket searching for her phone, at the same time she reached for the door handle.

The lights flickered back on, and she breathed a sigh of relief.

Not sure whether to feel silly, scared, or annoyed Emma picked up her bag and walked into the house. It smelled musty. If she was honest, it smelt of old ladies. Of lavender and of damp. The furniture was old and dark as was most of the room. Wood paneling lined the walls, and the ceiling rose three stories with a balcony on each level. It made the room seem dark and imposing even with the meager light. There were four doors going off the hallway, and she walked towards the first one.

With relief, she found the kitchen. Everything would feel better with a cup of tea. This room smelt different, and as she flicked on the lights, she saw a potted plant growing in the window. It was a vibrant green with purple flowers and seemed to be the only color in the dark and dreary room. Next to it was a small brass bell. She lifted the plant to her nose and recognized the scent. It was Sage. Well, she guessed she had a herb for cooking.

Soon the kettle was boiling, and she started to look around the kitchen. The cupboards held just a few cans. The labels were peeling, the metal rusty, she found a bin bag and gathered them all together. On the work surface was a bread bin. Opening it, she almost gagged. The scent of mold was intense, and inside was a bag that appeared to have grown a new lifeform. Lifting the bin, she took it outside, through a small porch that was shrouded with trees. They scraped their bare branches against the glass squealing and shrieking in a manner that set her nerves on edge. Wiping her hands, she dumped the bread bin in the waste and ran back into the kitchen.

Tea made, she decided to look around the house. It was so quiet, and for a moment she thought maybe she should get a dog or a cat. It would be nice to have something to talk to, some company.

On a small table in the hallway, she found another envelope. Excitement surged through her for she recognized the writing. Tearing it open she found a card from Lynn. Suddenly there were tears in her eyes. How would she cope without her friend, her mentor?

The card was typical of Lynn. A big bunch of balloons was resplendent on the front along with Congratulations on Your New Home.

Was it a home? Not yet, but maybe one day.

The writing inside was bright, bubbly, and congratulating her on the big step she had taken. On leaving the shelter and starting a new life. It felt like her friend had reached across the miles and given her a hug, she could do this, she could start again.

***

After a good hour of exploring, Emma had brought in her few possessions. It was just her clothes, toiletries, the gifts from the shelter, and her laptop. There was no television, so she decided to Skype with Lynn. On the ground floor, there was a small living room. A fire to one side was burning brightly, after only three attempts and one scolded finger.

The walls of the room were lined with dusty old books. A beige flower covered, small, and slightly moth eared sofa was directly opposite the fire. It had given her quite a shock when she first came into the room. On one end was a black cat curled around on itself. The door had been shut, how long had it been there? Tentatively, Emma had reached out to touch the animal. It did not move, and she gave a sharp laugh. It was one of those ornaments that looked so real. It was simply fake fur surrounding a heavy, sawdust covered shape.

Matching old lady chairs sat either side of the sofa. Emma was about to sit in the one facing away from the door. Something stopped her, she turned and sat in the one facing the door.

The house was so quiet, and it was unnerving her. So she fired up her laptop, put on some headphones, and opened up Skype.

The screen flashed at her. No connection.

"Oh, this is just peachy," she said and a sudden urge to throw the laptop across the room overtook her.

Taking a breath, she browsed to her music and opened a file of alpha wave recordings from the center. It would provide background noise and help her relax and concentrate, and hopefully, it would improve her confidence.

For the next hour, Emma worked on her laptop. She had a few copywriting assignments for different companies. Some were in London, some were international. It was a job that Lynn had set up for her, and she loved it. What's more, it gave her the chance to work from home. Once she got the internet sorted she would never have to leave the house unless she wanted to. Only that was her old self talking, it was not a future. Suddenly, she missed Lynn, and a wave of fatigue ran through her. Closing the laptop, she decided on a glass of wine, a quick shower, and bed.

The bedroom she had chosen was at the back of the house and decorated in a pale rose color. Under the weak lamp, it looked wishy-washy in places and yet blood red over the bed. For a moment she was creeped out. Shaking off the feeling she took a sip of chardonnay and pulled her sweatshirt up and over her head. At that moment, the one when it was covering her eyes and tangled around her arms she heard a child's scream. It pierced the air and shocked her to the bone.

"Shit!" she called as the sweatshirt tied up her arms and stuck to her hair. Flailing, she yanked and pulled as she stumbled around the room. Trying to remember where the bed and dresser were. For long moments the material stuck, but she could hear nothing more. No more screams, no footsteps, just the blood racing in her ears and her own desperate breathing.

The shirt pulled free, and she stared at the room. The closet door had come open, and it leered at her, a black hole full of...

"Stop it!" she admonished herself.

This was silly, the scream would just be some kids playing in the woods behind the house. They were the sort of place you went with a few cans and a few friends. No doubt they had built a fire and were sat on logs telling each other tall tales. That was all she had heard... and yet the hairs stood proudly on her arms, and her heart was pounding like a racing horse.

The closet door moved away from her, and she backed away.

What was happening?

With her heart in her throat, she

approached the door. It was a room she had been pleased to find when she checked out the bedroom. A walk in wardrobe with rails, shelves and just a few creepy old clothes hanging there. Quickly, she had bundled them up into some black bags. Then she had unpacked her own few clothes and hung them up in the closet. It had made her feel important, yet she did not know why. Just two dresses, three pairs of jeans and a few tops was hardly a wardrobe.

The door moved again.

Stopping in her tracks she wondered what she should do, could someone be in there? Then she heard Lynn's voice. Calmly telling her that things would unnerve her, that she should expect it and face up to them.

Heart pounding and with her breath trapped in her chest, she approached the door. As she passed the window, a draft lifted her hair and eased her nerves. The window! It was slightly open. That must have been what caused the door to move. Why was she being so stupid? Letting out a bark of nervous laughter she pulled the door closed and slid across the bolt. Why was there a bolt on the outside of the closet?

Feeling a little better she closed the window and drew the thin curtains, shutting out the shadows from the trees behind. Booting up her laptop she pulled the headphones out and put on the same music as before. At least it would hide the creaks and groans of the old wood while she had her shower.

Moving her head from side to side she took her right hand and tried to ease out the kinks in her neck. It had been a long day. As she began to take off her t-shirt. A noise seemed to shake the house.

KNOCK, KNOCK, KNOCK.

Emma froze, and a sob came to her throat.

It had happened. Her worst nightmare. Right then she wanted to open the cupboard door, crawl inside and hide in the corner. How could this happen? She had been so careful. Lynn had been so careful and yet...

The knock came again. A small yelp came from her throat as she jumped. What could she do? The house was so remote, she wanted to hide, but the door seemed to beckon her to it. Running a hand through her long brown hair, she shoved it over her shoulders, grabbed something from her bag, and walked to the stairs. The hallway light was on, but it barely reached the second level. Maybe she could hide?

No, it wouldn't work. If he had found her address, then he would not give in. She had to do what Lynn told her and face her demons.

With each step her legs felt like lead and yet she pushed back her shoulders and strolled to the door. With her right hand poised behind her back, she pulled it open. Quickly, she raised her right hand and pointed the can of mace right into the eyes of a very surprised delivery man holding a big bunch of brightly colored flowers. At the last moment, she managed to not depress the button and sobbing, she dropped her hand. Much to the relief of the man before her.

"Delivery for Emma," he said.

Relieved and embarrassed Emma took the flowers and the three bags of groceries that the man had brought.

Searching the cupboards, she found an old jug and placed the beautiful chrysanthemums in it. The groceries were packed away, and she opened the card.

I knew you would forget to get any food. Welcome to your new home. Stay strong and know that you can do this.

Ring me anytime you need to talk.

Love Lynn.

Emma smiled and held the card to her chest. She was so lucky to have such a good friend. Quickly, she made herself a sandwich. Then collecting her glass of wine from the lounge, she made up the fire. Behind her the sofa was empty, but she did not notice the cat was no longer there. Feeling happy and just a little silly about her panic attacks, Emma went to bed.

Caroline Clark

Chapter Three

First thing in the morning Emma made herself a quick breakfast. Then she took the car and drove into Castleton, it being a 25-minute drive, and the twisty roads made her feel tired and grumpy. When she got there, she rang Lynn and was so relieved to hear her friend's voice.

"It's good to hear from you," Lynn said. "I was starting to worry last night, but then I know you, you can cope with anything, and I believe in you."

Emma felt her throat clench and tears formed in her eyes, she bit them back and swallowed. "It's so good to hear from you Lynn. The house is a little creepy, and there is no phone or the Internet, and my mobile doesn't work there either. Maybe this was a bad decision. I was just thinking..." Emma stopped, if she said what she thought Lynn would feel that she had failed. The last thing she wanted to do was disappoint her friend. "I guess I'm just a bit nervous out on my own. You are right, I can do this, and I have you to thank for that, my friend."

The rest of the conversation was simply Emma and Lynn catching up. She had made a decision she could do this, and she was going to make a go of it. Although the house was creepy, it was old, dark and empty, and it was not hers... well, it was hers, but it didn't feel like it... not at the moment. But it would do, given time, she could make a go of this. Feeling better she set off for the local library, and there downloaded some jobs and checked on her emails. Once the work was done, she could go back to the house and not need to leave it for at least another four or five days. So she took a little time to explore the beautiful quaint shops and the wonderful countryside. When she arrived the night before, she hadn't had time to appreciate the majestic beauty of the surrounding hills. It was a picture postcard of green mounds and lowly dales, and she couldn't believe her luck.

***

Emma arrived back at the house just before lunch. So she made herself a sandwich and a coffee and ate them in front of the fire. She hadn't made it this morning, but the house was warm, and she didn't think she would need to until later that night. There was plenty of wood in a basket on the hearth, and she had found a store outside, with lots more, along with a creepy old axe.

After her lunch, she opened up her laptop and worked on copy for a website for the next couple of hours. Suddenly, she felt tired and closed the laptop. Leaning back in the chair she closed her eyes for just a second. Lynn had included a bottle of hot chocolate in the groceries. Suddenly, she felt homesick. For the times they would sit up late into the night drinking hot chocolate and talking. Yet, she was also so tired, the long drive, the stress, and panic had all taken it out on her. So she let her shoulders relax, and before she knew it, she had fallen asleep in the chair.

Something touched her leg, it was so brief so slight she was not sure it had even happened. Her eyes flicked open but she was so comfortable she did not want to wake. Closing her eyes again she relaxed back down and ignored it. Just five more minutes and she would get a drink. A shudder ran down her spine, and goose bumps rose on her arms. The room was suddenly so cold she started to shiver, and again something touched her leg. In a flash, her hand went down to bat it away, but there was nothing there. She jerked awake and jumped out of the chair, almost tossing her laptop onto the floor.

The room was cold, really cold, and she could still feel the trace of something across her leg. Something silky, like animal fur. The house was dark.

How long had she slept?

Suddenly, she felt afraid and yet, also very silly. Was she just panicking again? Of course, it was cold, the sun had gone down.

The feeling in my legs?

Then she almost laughed, she had been asleep in a chair, of course, her legs felt strange, silly, they had gone to sleep. It was just the blood rushing back into them.

The light in the room did not seem bright enough, so she walked out of the door and put on the hall light. The hall seemed warmer.

Why was that?

Suddenly, she needed a drink, and this time it was not going to be hot chocolate. She made her way across the hall towards the kitchen. As she went beneath the banister a silky thread traced across her face. Her hand shot up to swipe it away, as her heart galloped like a racing horse. The tendril seemed to cling to her. The more she swiped at it, the more it stuck to her face and neck. It was hard to breathe, her chest ached, and her throat felt as if something was digging into it. A shadow passed before her seeming to coalesce before her eyes. A dark shadow! Then it was gone and so was whatever she had walked into.

Emma stood there, dropped her head, grabbed onto her knees, and breathed heavily. What was happening? The house was so quiet, so lonely, and so empty and she was filled with fear.

What was here, what was causing this?

Maybe she couldn't do this, maybe she

should just leave. Then she saw Lynn's card. The bright balloons, and the second card alongside the flowers. It brought her back to reason. There was no need to panic, there was no need to look for silly reasons. Looking down at her hands she realized that she had walked into a cobweb... just a cobweb and yet she had experienced a major panic attack.

"Get a hold of yourself, Emma," she said to the empty house.

The sound of trees hitting the window on the first landing drew her eyes. As the trees shook and waved their skeletal branches in the wind, they caused shadows to jump against the walls. It was all just her nerves!

This was just her getting used to a new situation. Getting used to being alone. She had left Mark, and she had survived, now she had left the shelter, and she would survive this. She would get used to living alone and soon she would enjoy it. She made a note to plug in her iPlayer and fill the house with music. It was creepy because it was all so quiet. So different to a home filled with 20 of her friends.

Feeling better she walked into the kitchen opened the fridge and poured herself a glass of wine. Taking a large sip, she looked out the window. The back of the property was surrounded by woods. There was no fence, no nothing, it just drifted off into the trees, and more of them crowded around the back door. Maybe that was why she felt a little bit insecure.

Taking another sip of wine, she relished the crisp sharpness as it hit the back of her throat. The trees tap, tap, tapped against the window. Maybe she should get out there and cut them back?

Turning, she walked out of the kitchen and across the hall. Looking at her watch, it was not late, only just past ten and yet she felt so very tired. Taking the wine she put on the heating, it was too late to light the fire. The house ticked and creaked as the pipes warmed up. Ignoring it, she climbed the stairs and took a quick shower.

The water was warm and relaxing, and she felt so much better after a quick soak. Taking her wine, she left the hall light on and climbed into bed. There she opened a book on her mobile and began to read. Soon her eyes would not stay open. Putting down the phone she turned off the light and curled under the duvet. It felt cool but safe. She closed her eyes and slept.

Emma did not see, but in front of the cupboard, was the stuffed black cat. It looked so real, so peaceful and yet, as if it could move at any moment.

Caroline Clark

Chapter Four

Emma woke from a fitful sleep to find the house freezing. Quickly, she grabbed her robe. It was soft and fluffy and a candy floss pink. A present from Lynn when she first came to the shelter. It wrapped her in a comforting warmth as she ran down the wooden stairs to put on the heating.

Then she jumped in the shower as the house began to heat up. The water was lukewarm, but it would do, and it freshened her up. Sat on the bed, she began to dress. Strange ticking noises made her look behind her, then there was a creaking, groaning, and she felt her heart start to pound. Yet she knew it was just the pipes. As the house heated up, they were bound to make noises. After all, it was an old house and had not been lived in for some months.

Feeling better she went to the kitchen and made herself some toast and tea. Stood in the kitchen she could feel a draft behind her. It was not the first time she turned around to see where it came from. The wall behind her was roughly plastered and painted in whitewash. As she watched, the white faded, darkened and a stain appeared. It was spreading like a living thing. Like some black mold that was filmed in slow motion and seemed to grow before her very eyes. She raised her hand to her face and felt her mouth open. "What the..."

As soon as it had appeared, the stain was gone, and the wall was simply a faded white again. Emma clasped onto the worktop and tried to control her breathing. Was she seeing things? The sound of a bang behind her had her jumping around. Her heart in her throat, she felt her knees go weak. Somebody was there. A shadow passed across the window, a light shape and then it was gone.

Emma moved towards the door, her hand was shaking, was someone there? The sound of laughter behind her was high-pitched, almost like a child and she could smell smoke. She flipped back around. No one was in the kitchen. It was if the noise was coming from within the walls. Had she heard it? She began to question herself, for the noise had just been on the edge of her hearing.

Knock, knock, knock.

Emma jumped, and a hand flew to her mouth. She stood there, frightened, her knees weak, her stomach turning, and the hairs on the back of her arms standing on edge. Once again her mind turned to Mark. Had he found her?

The knock came again, only this time she could see a shape through the glass panel of the back door. Someone was there, someone was inside the porch.

"Hello," came a woman's voice.

Relief flooded through Emma, and she gasped out loud. Quickly, she walked to the door and opened it to see a woman stood there. A basket was thrust towards her, full of muffins, and Emma reached out to grab it.

"Morning, I'm Janet... I just wanted to see how you were doing, if you had settled in?"

Emma fumbled with the basket and stepped backward indicating to Janet to come in. Tree branches scratched against the porch windows like chalk on a blackboard or nails on glass.

Janet had shoulder length brown hair cut into a bob that swung as she moved. Rosy red cheeks told of the nip in the air, and big brown eyes looked surprised over a friendly smile.

"I heard somebody was moving in. I just wanted to see how you are doing," Janet said again.

Emma was still trying to control the pounding of her heart, but she put the basket on the side and indicated a small table in the corner. Janet took a seat. The smile on her face hadn't slipped once.

"Would you like a drink?" Emma asked. "Oh, I'm Emma, by the way, and it's nice to meet you."

Janet nodded. "Tea would be lovely."

"Do you live nearby?" Emma asked as she put on the kettle.

"I'm your nearest neighbor. It's about 5 miles away."

Emma gulped, so far.

Soon she had made the drinks and they

were sitting and eating raspberry muffins. It felt nice to have someone there, to have noise in the house and to not feel alone. Maybe that had been the problem all along, maybe it was just being all alone. As they drank and ate, Emma could not help but notice that Janet always had a smile on her face.

"Did you know my aunt?" Emma asked.

Janet put down her cup, and it rattled on the table. Emma notice that the smile had gone from her face.

"I didn't know her well, I don't think anyone did. Did you know her?"

Emma shook her head. "I didn't even know she existed... Not until I got the letter telling me about this house. I can't explain how happy I was. To be given this chance and this place... it was just amazing." The words sounded hollow in her mouth and to her ears. It was an amazing house, an amazing opportunity, and yet she just felt like she wanted to leave. To run back to the city, to run back to her friends.

"I can imagine that would be quite a shock," Janet said as she fiddled with her hands on the table. "Did you find the letter Sylvia left you?"

Emma shook her head confused. "All I got was a letter from the solicitor."

Janet looked across at the work surface as if she was searching for something. "She told me she'd left it on the side or if not it would be in the bread bin. I think you really ought to read it."

Why did that sound so ominous? Emma thought and then she shuddered. "In the bread bin!"

Janet nodded.

Emma remembered the moldy bread smell from the bread bin and yet, now it looked like she would have to dig it out of the rubbish to find this letter. Did it matter?

The two of them talked another 10 to 15 minutes, drinking tea and eating muffins. Janet invited her to a party she was having with a few friends in a couple of weeks, and Emma said that she would come.

"I sometimes hear a child laughing or possibly even screaming," Emma said, hoping that she did not sound too silly.

"It could be children playing in the woods," Janet said, her eyebrows were knitted together, and she did not seem convinced.

"The house is strange too, there are cold drafts, strange noises. I know. it's silly, but I felt like somebody touched my leg the other night." Emma did not know why she was saying these things. She knew what was happening, she was stressed, looking for trouble where there was none. Apart from that, she didn't

even know this woman yet she was admitting
to being scared in front of her.

Janet seemed to be studying her fingers.
They were small and neat, her nails perfectly
polished in a pearlescent shade of pink. Emma
got the feeling she wanted to say something.

"What is it?" she asked.

"You need to read that letter," Janet said.
"Maybe Sylvia will explain... you see... well...
there are rumors about this house. Some say it
is haunted. Some say the spirit of a child who
was burnt in the garden out back still haunts
this place... that it has not been laid to rest."
Janet gave a light laugh as if she was mocking
herself. "I can't believe I just said that. It's
obviously really silly, and I don't mean to scare
you." She pulled out a notepad from her pocket
and wrote down a phone number passing it to
Emma. "If you ever need anything just give me
a call, now, I really have to be going. It was nice
to meet you, Emma." Janet stood and walked

to the door. "I usually go to Castleton once a week, why don't I pick you up next Thursday."

Emma nodded and then watched as her friend picked up the empty basket and walked out of the door. Suddenly, the house was very empty again. Very empty and very ominous. She stood in the kitchen looking out the window. Suddenly, the haunting sound of a child's scream came from behind her. As she turned, a cold draft hit her face and lifted her hair, it smelt of smoke and clogged her throat. With fear clenching an icy hand onto her heart, Emma turned. The house was so silent as if it was waiting. All she could hear was a high-pitched whine, as if her ears had been subjected to an explosion. A stream of mist appeared before her as her breath turned to vapor in the frosty air. "Sh..." she tried to say the cuss word but nothing came out, her throat would not move, and she was shivering with the cold.

Suddenly, her ears popped as if the pressure had changed and the room was warm. The sound of the pipes ticking released the spell and she sagged back against the counter.

What was going on?

Caroline Clark

Chapter Five

Emma knew she must get the letter out of the bread bin. It was not something she was looking forward to, and so she pulled some rubber gloves out of the cupboard and taking the last sip of tea she steeled herself for the task ahead. It wasn't hard to get hold of the bread bin, she pulled it up and out of the bin. Taking a breath, she opened the flap. The site of the moldy bread almost made her gag, and the smell seemed to clog at the back of her throat. She reached in and grabbed hold of the bag pulling it straight out and back into the big bin. There at the back was a plastic sleeve. Emma pulled it out and could see a letter inside of it. Once she had the letter, she threw the bread bin back into the trash, pulled off the rubber gloves and threw them after it. Slamming the lid, she returned to the kitchen.

Once she had washed her hands, she sat down at the table and pulled the letter out of the plastic. It was folded over but in a neat script on the top was just one word. *Emma.* Taking a breath, she opened the letter.

My dearest Emma,

I know you do not know me, but I am your aunt. My name is Sylvia, and I have lived in this house all my life. There has been a member of our family in this house since it was built in 1575 and there must be one until the end of time.

I have to tell you some harsh truths. One of our family was killed here, and since that time one of us has remained to see that justice is done. Now it is your turn. Do not allow visitors to enter this house. Do not allow anyone into the cage. The longer you stay here, the more you will see, the more you will feel. The presence of your great-great-great-grandmother, Ursula Kemp, will give you strength and let you see.

There is evil in this house, and it is your job to make sure that it does not escape. Mark my words, evil is here, and if you let it, it will leave. The consequences of that will be grave for all.

I wish I could be here with you, to explain what you need to do, but I cannot. My time has come, but maybe we will meet soon. Maybe I will be strong enough to help you. There will be times when you will be afraid. There may be times when you will be in danger. Do not underestimate Alden Carter, for he committed a crime that can never be forgiven. If he can, he will hurt you, if he can, he will kill you. Do not trust the young girl. Though she was a victim, evil runs through her veins. She is not the one to protect, she must be kept here and never allowed to leave.

Rely on your relatives, rely on those who came before and rely on Ursula, for only she can keep you safe.

Look after the cat for he has been here as long as I have.

Sylvia.

Emma stared at the letter for a long time not knowing quite what to think. Surely her aunt must have lost her mind. Maybe it was dementia, or maybe it was just some sickness brought on by old age and loneliness. Whatever it was the letter had left Emma feeling disturbed and wanting to get out of the house even for just a little while. Maybe she should go into Castleton and have a coffee. Maybe just getting out of the house for a while would make her feel better. Then she remembered she had a deadline. Tomorrow she was supposed to turn in some work. One more hour and she could finish it. So, she decided to spend that time, finish the work, and then get out of the house at least for a couple of hours. Maybe just being around other people would give her time to think.

Emma lit the fire, not because it was cold but simply because it gave her the feeling of not being alone. Then she fired up her laptop and started on her work. Soon she was engrossed and was starting to forget the bad feeling she had. It was silly to think that the house was haunted and the letter from her aunt was just plain stupid. There was no way she was going to let it spoil things for her.

It took just over an hour to complete the copywriting work. She saved it to her hard drive, typed up an email, attached the work, and then realized she couldn't send it. Of course, the Internet still wasn't working so she would have to go into town, check on the Internet, have a coffee, call Lynn, and send off her work. Then she would come back for the night. The thought of that sent a shiver down her spine, she shook it away. Nothing had happened, nothing was going to happen.

Closing her laptop, she walked to the kitchen for her coat. As she grabbed it from a chair, she noticed the stuffed cat curled up on the counter. The coat dropped from her hand.

"Jesus!"

Her heart was pounding, the hair was stood up on the back of her neck, and her knees felt like jelly. How had it gotten in here? The last time she remembered, it was on the sofa, looking all creepy and real.

This had to be a joke.

Someone had to be playing a joke on her.

Was it Janet? Had she ever left her alone?

Emma knew she hadn't, and the words of the letter came back to haunt her. Sylvia had written, "look after the cat for he has been here as long as I have."

Emma felt as if she was going to start to laugh, but it would not be a laugh of joy, it would be a hysterical laugh that she knew would take over if she let it. As she walked towards the stuffed cat, its black fur all shiny and real, a loud bang sounded from the front of the house. Emma did not know which way to turn. She did not want to turn away from the cat, afraid of what it may do and yet she knew that was crazy. Still, she ran for the front door and yanked it open. A shadow disappeared into the woods. She could not see who it was or even what it was, but something had been there.

That was it, she had to get out of here. Grabbing her car keys, she locked the doors and ran through the trees until she could lock herself inside the secure comfort of the Volvo.

Soon she was in Castleton and sat in a coffee shop. With the sound of conversation all around her and the sun shining through the windows all of a sudden, it all seemed so silly. Yet she had to talk to somebody, and so she rang Lynn.

It had been so good to talk to Lynn and to catch up, her friend's words kept ringing in her ears.

"Go to the police," Lynn had said. "This may be nothing, but you do not know. Let someone come over and check things out for you. And don't forget, if you need anything, call me."

Emma was on her 3rd cup of coffee, feeling more and more jittery by the second. She knew that Lynn was right, it would not hurt to go to the police. Maybe they knew of someone who was playing tricks in the area. Maybe it was Mark. Either way, it wouldn't hurt to get things checked out. It would make her feel better. So she finished off the work she had to do, checked her emails once more and then googled the local police station. It was just a five-minute walk, so she decided to leave the car. Yet the closer she got to the station the more foolish she felt. What had she actually seen? Would they laugh at her?

Caroline Clark

Chapter Six

Emma could feel the sun on her back as she walked next to a gentle stream. It burbled and glittered and looked so normal and so serene that she wondered if she was going mad. *Had any of this happened?*

It did not matter, Lynn was right, and she would report it and then see what happened. Maybe some teenager had broken into the house, moved the cat and then knocked on the door to scare her... maybe.

As she walked along a robin hopped onto the pavement in front of her. Its red breast was resplendent, and it cocked its head and gave her a cheeky look. For a moment she laughed.

If only life was so simple as to be begging for scraps in the sunshine. The bird jumped at her laughter and then flew away as if it realized she was a lost cause.

Emma pulled her eyes from the stream and looked around. The stone houses were set close to the road, and in places, the path was very narrow. There was not much traffic, it was only March and the tourist season had not really started yet. So the village had a lazy feel, and she began to relax. Passing a shop offering cream teas, she decided to try one next time. Maybe she could persuade Janet to join her? Next was a shop selling souvenirs and then a hiking store. Emma decided that maybe she should get some boots, and why not a dog? The idea was a good one. A dog would keep her company and get her out of the house, maybe she would go to the pound, if there was one locally.

Suddenly, she thought of the creepy black

cat. How had it moved into the kitchen? Someone had to be playing a prank.

The police station was an old building with big double doors that seemed to weigh a ton. Pushing through she saw a small room with a counter. A man in a slate gray suit was stood with his back to her.

"May I help you," he asked as he turned around.

He was tall, with short and tousled rich brown hair. Blue eyes seemed to glow above dimpled cheeks and a nice smile.

Emma felt suddenly confused. "I was after a policeman," she said and instantly blushed. *What a stupid thing to say!*

"At your service, ma'am, Detective Inspector Brent Markham." He bowed and smiled even more.

Emma felt heat hit her cheeks and she

wanted to turn and run. It was not an attraction that made her cheeks glow, but anger. How dare this man think he could charm her? Perhaps something in her expression warned him of her feelings for his smile slipped off his face and he pointed towards the door.

"Come this way, and we can talk."

Emma followed him along a narrow and scuff-marked corridor to a small room. There were a few seats, a sofa, and a drinks machine. It smelt of stale coffee and cleaning fluid but looked clean if a little tatty.

"Take a seat," he said. "Let me get you a coffee."

Emma wanted to say no but thought that maybe it would be better if she had something to hold. As long as she didn't throw it at him.

Brent placed two cups on the table and

took out a notepad. "Now Miss, tell me what the problem is."

Emma suddenly felt relaxed, and so she told him. About the strange feelings, that something had touched her leg, the screams she had heard, the knocks on the door, the smell of smoke and the moving cat. Once she had finished it all sounded so small, so inconsequential, and so stupid. She really was losing it and yet he just nodded.

"Is there anything else you want to tell me?" he asked.

There was something about his tone that made her want to talk. Maybe it was his training for she would never trust a man, not again. Yet she told him about Mark. How he had broken her collarbone and arm. How he had beaten her until she was unconscious and put her in the hospital. How he had tried to find her and swore that if he did she would pay. "He couldn't have found me... could he?"

Brent looked up from his notes, and there was only warmth and understanding in his eyes. "I don't think so, but I will have him checked out."

Emma felt her heart jump in her chest. "Don't do that, he will trace me here."

"No, he won't. No one will know where the inquiry comes from." Brent smiled, but it was no longer flirtatious, just reassuring and calm. "Don't worry, we have dealt with this sort of situation before. The call goes to a central station, and they pass information on to his local force. They will check on him and report back via the chain. There is no way he can trace you. Now, I will come back with you. Check over the house and surrounding area and see if I can spot if anyone has been playing pranks. Why don't I drive you back to your car?"

Emma wanted to refuse. Surely, this was not the case for a detective inspector? Yet somehow she could not refuse for no one else would believe her.

***

The journey back to her car was difficult for Emma. Sitting so close to another man brought back all her old fears. Brent seemed to realize this, he didn't speak much, kept his eyes on the road and just let her be. It was relaxing, and she appreciated the gesture.

Soon he was following her down the tight twisty roads and eventually she turned onto the lane that led down to Brynlee House. It seemed to rear out of the trees, and the moment she set eyes on the place, she felt a deep disquiet.

"This is my house, Detective Inspector Markham. What do we do now?" For a second she thought she saw amusement in his blue eyes, but he kept his face neutral and nodded towards the door.

"Let's go inside and have a look around. You can show me what happened."

Emma nodded and led the way beneath the trees, along the path, and into the house. The first thing she did was take him to the kitchen. The cat was nowhere to be seen! "There!" she pointed at the work surface. "The cat was there. I swear it to you." Emma gulped down some air. She could feel panic growing inside of her. Maybe it was being all alone in the house with a big strong man. Maybe it was the fear that she was going mad. Maybe it was just worry that everything was too much for her and that she would never escape her past.

"I believe you," he said. "Let's have a look round."

Emma shivered as a cold draft seemed to envelope her. She turned towards the wall expecting to see the stain growing there. There was nothing. Ignoring the feeling she led him back to the hallway. Then into the little lounge.

There on the sofa, as if it had never moved, was the stuffed cat. She felt her breath catch in her throat. Had she just imagined it all? A shaky hand pointed towards the sofa. This time she was sure that Brent had to stifle a laugh, he didn't believe her.

Brent moved towards the cat, and Emma felt a sudden fear. What if it attacked him? Then she realized what a stupid thing she was thinking. She must have imagined it. After all, the cat had really freaked her out. Maybe it was just a shadow on the counter, and she had seen what she wanted to see.

Brent reached out a hand and stroked the black fur. "It really does look real," he said as he turned to face her.

It appeared to move beneath his fingers, Brent jumped back with a yelp. Emma didn't know whether to laugh or scream. A chill went through her, and the room seemed so cold. As she breathed her breath misted before her. The cat jumped from the sofa, brushing her leg as it disappeared from the room.

Emma could hardly move. The feeling on her leg, where the cat brushed past. That was the exact sensation she had felt before. Could the damned cat have been alive all along? It didn't make sense. The house had been empty for several weeks. Surely the cat would have died. Yet there it was, it had run away. How could she be so stupid?

"Well, that's one mystery solved," Brent said with a big smile on his face.

"I don't understand." Emma was pointing at the sofa feeling rather silly just stood there as she tried to comprehend what happened. "It wasn't real. I swear to you it wasn't real." As she spoke her breath misted before her, and she noticed Brent looking at it. His right eyebrow rose, but he never said a word. Instead, he pointed to the door and led her back into the hallway.

Emma noticed it was warmer here. Suddenly, she was desperate for a drink, and she walked into the kitchen. In the fridge was the remains of the bottle of wine but it was too early for that and even if it wasn't, she was drinking too much. "You must think I'm just crazy."

"This house definitely has a vibe," Brent said. "I'm a detective, so let's detect, let's see what's going on. Apart from the moving cat you heard voices and said there were cold spots. It was definitely strange in that room, I saw your breath. Why don't you put the kettle on while I go back in there and see what I can find?"

Emma nodded. Maybe he didn't believe her but at least he wasn't laughing, and it felt good to not be alone. While Emma made some coffees, Brent left the room. She could hear him walking about, knocking on walls, moving pictures, looking at books on the bookshelf. What did he expect to find? Emma had no idea, but maybe a new perspective on things would help.

Soon she had two steaming mugs of coffee, and she placed them on the table. Her back was to the window of the door. She was facing the wall that sometimes changed color, facing where the draft came from. The sound of laughter, child's laughter came from behind that wall, and the air was filled with smoke. Emma froze. She had to know what it was, had to find out who was doing this and she tried to call Brent, but the words would not come. There was a lump in her throat, a tightness there, and she could not speak.

As she tried to swallow, the laughter changed to a scream, and the temperature in the room dropped at least 10°. Emma felt her teeth chatter, and she began to shiver and yet she could not move. The scream grew louder and then softer, she was almost in tears as Brent ran into the room.

"I heard it," he said. "I heard it too."

Emma was staring at the wall, for that was where she had heard the noise. "Maybe somebody is trapped... or outside... maybe this is just a recording... a prank." She was fighting back the tears and trying to remain calm. Someone had heard it, she was not going mad... this was real.

Brent looked a little shaken, his face was paler, but it still held a smile. Then he turned away from the wall and looked towards the door. Unlocking the door, he pulled it open. The draft came in through the dilapidated old porch. Brent began to laugh.

Emma turned angry. What was he laughing at? Then she heard the noise again, it sounded different now without the door muffling it. There were trees and bushes growing close to the porch. The bare branches poked out towards the glass. Skeletal fingers were scratching against the window. As they shook in the wind, the noise rose and fell in time with the branches.

How could she have been so stupid?

Heat hit her cheeks, and she knew she was blushing. "I am so sorry to have wasted your time," she said. Though she had an explanation for the noises she had heard, still she felt uneasy.

Brent opened the door from the porch to the outside. As he did, the black cat ran past him and into the house. It was fast, just a streak of fur, just a black shadow. Brent turned and gave her a smile, as he did, an almighty bang sounded behind him. Brent let go of the door and jumped around.

Again he laughed, only this time it was a mighty peel, and it sounded genuine. Emma peered around to see behind him. A sturdy tree grew this side and when the wind really blew it thumped into the side of the house.

"You must think I'm hysterical?" she said as she stumbled to the table and sat down.

"No, I don't," Brent said as he joined her in the seat opposite. "We have found explanations for some of the things, and I think maybe you were just a little scared. That is understandable, and there is nothing to be ashamed of. I'm not working this weekend, why don't I come over and cut down some of those branches, and you can let me know about anything else that happened."

This time he was smiling broader, more confident and she felt more heat warm her cheeks.

"Would you really do that for me?" she asked

"I'm looking forward to it."

Emma was filled with relief. He would come back, and she would be safe, then another fear surfaced. The fear of trusting. The fear of being under the control of a man. "This is not a date," she blurted out and felt her voice shake. "I want you to understand I'm not... I'm just not ready.

Chapter Seven

The moment Brent left, the house felt empty and oppressive again. Emma grabbed herself a glass of wine and went into the small living room. The cat was curled up on the sofa. Once again it looked stuffed. Taking a gulp from her wine, she put the glass down and approached it. "So, kitty, are you alive?"

Emma almost laughed at the absurdity of her comment. The cat raised its head, opened its eyes, and stared at her. There was something creepy about its amber gaze, and she could not return it. She turned her back on the cat and set about preparing a fire. Soon it was burning nicely, and she picked up her laptop and sat down in the chair. There was still no Internet, and she did not feel like working, so she put on some music and closed her eyes.

As soon as her eyes were closed, the hairs on her arms stood up, her breath caught in her throat and her stomach dropped as her thoughts returned to the cat. Could it really have been alive all this time? She tried to think back, tried to imagine how it had felt, and she was sure it had been stuffed. The fur was soft but cold, and the body was hard and solid. It felt like... sawdust. Yet, when Brent touched it, it moved. It ran from the house and then it ran back in. Yet, if it was alive what had it eaten? Then she saw the absurdity of the whole situation. It was a cat, it probably had its own entrance and exit into the house. No doubt it spent the night hunting and didn't need her to feed it. Only now, if it was going to live here, she would feed it. The last thing she wanted to do was wake up to find a mouse on her bed.

The nagging feeling that something was wrong was eating at the back of her mind. Only she didn't want to hear it, not now, she just wanted a normal night, time to relax. So she pushed the sensation of touching the cat to the back of her mind. Maybe it was old, and that was the reason it didn't move too much.

Emma decided to make herself some toast, she got up and went into the kitchen. The cat followed, and as it passed, she felt a cold draft against her legs. Shaking off the feeling she grabbed some bread and set about making the toast. The cat jumped onto the work surface. Emma gasped and jumped backward. Instinctively her hand moved out to bat it away. She touched its body and almost gagged. It was as if she was touching a sawdust-stuffed bag coated in cat hair.

What was happening to her?

The cat meowed and jumped back up onto the surface. Emma was not going to touch it again. The last thing she wanted to do was feel that solid, inanimate body. So instead, she reached into the cupboard and pulled out a can of tuna. Soon the fish was piled into a dish, and she placed it on the floor. The cat gave her a look of pure disdain and then hopped off the surface. It strutted across to the dish, its tail held high like a flag. Emma watched as it sniffed the food and licked its lips. It turned to face her and gave her such a look of regret, of sadness... before walking out of the kitchen.

"I guess you don't like fish," Emma said.

Outside, the branches scratched on the window. They no longer sounded exactly like laughter or screams, but if she closed her eyes, they were so close. Now they no longer terrified her but still set her nerves on edge. The toast was done, so she scraped on some jam and went back to sit beside the fire. The cat was curled up in its normal place, and the room was cold. She stoked up the fire and sat down to eat her toast and finish her glass of wine.

Closing her eyes, she tried to think through everything that had happened. The more she thought about it, the more she knew it must be her nerves. What other rational explanation was there? Soon she had drifted off to sleep, and she woke to the feeling of something touching her leg. Instinctively she jerked away, but there was nothing there. Eyes wide, heart pounding, she sat up and searched the room. It was dark now, and there was just a faint glow from the fire. It didn't chase away the shadows or show her the corners of the room and yet she could plainly see the cat sat on the sofa. It was watching her.

Could that be what touched her leg?

She reached down and rubbed where the feeling had been, pulling her hand up she could see cat hairs, and she almost laughed. Maybe she was just tired, it was time to go to bed.

Emma was dismayed that the cat followed her up the stairs. It wanted to come into the bedroom, but she would not let it, and firmly closed the door in its face. As she got into her night clothes, she could hear it meowing. Ignoring the plaintive cries, she jumped into bed, pulled the covers up over her ears and turned off the light.

It was some time later when she heard a soft noise. Still asleep, she could hear a voice. It was whispering and was just too low for her to understand. Ignoring the voice, she snuggled down deeper into the covers. Only the voice would not stop. It murmured, mumbled, and hissed away in her ear. Emma was too comfortable, she did not want to hear. Did not want to wake. Something told her to stay where she was. Then she felt something cold on her ear. It was like a tongue or the whisper of lips on her soft skin.

The voice was like a rustling, like leaves in

the cemetery and she could not understand it. There was a touch on her shoulder, and suddenly the words became clear.

"... go... goooo," the voice said dragging out the word until it became a threat. "... tooooo long. Someone .... or the deaths will continue."

Emma could only make out some of the words, and she mumbled in her sleep.

The lips moved closer, touching her ear once more and she could feel breath tickle her skin. Emma jerked awake and sat up in bed. It was dark, but she could feel something next to her. For a moment she was frozen. So afraid she could not even breathe. Yet she would not give in, she had never given into anything, and she would not start now. She reached out for the light, finding it the first time, the room was filled with the pale, sickly light that seemed to be a feature of the house. Staring at her were two glowing amber eyes filled with hatred and disdain.

Emma let out a squeal and jumped back in the bed pulling the covers up around her chin. The cat leaped from the bed and disappeared out of the room. Emma tried to watch where it had gone, only the door was still closed, and she could not see any point of egress.

She nudged her phone to check on the time, it was 2:30 AM. Too early to get up and yet she did not think she would sleep again. How had the cat got into the room? What was it doing on her bed? And what had she heard?

Emma dressed quickly and felt a little better in her jeans and a sweatshirt. Maybe this was all her imagination. The cat was just a cat, and like all cats, it got where it shouldn't. Being up and in the light, she was starting to feel a little better, so she decided to make a hot chocolate and just sit in the kitchen for a while.

As her hand reached for the bedroom door, she heard the child's scream.

"Shit!"

Heart pounding, she pulled her hand back as if it had been burned. "It's just the branches," she said. "Just the damned branches."

This time she grabbed hold of the handle, fear stayed her hand. What would be out there, what was waiting? Angry at her own nerves she yanked open the door. The wood paneled hallway was empty. Letting out a breath she walked from the room. Flicking on the lights as she rushed through the house. It was cold but not unnaturally so, this was just the normal chill of the early morning.

The movement made her feel better, and with every step she took, her confidence grew. Quickly, she skipped down the stairs, flicking on the light at the bottom. The hallway was still a depressing room, shadows flanked the corners, and the kitchen door was like a black gaping hole. For a moment she hesitated and then she felt as if hands touched her back. Launching her forwards, she stumbled, wheeled her arms and righted herself. Quickly, she spun around. There was nothing there. No one was there! Nothing had touched her and yet she could still feel the impression on her shoulders. Fear weakened her knees and trapped the breath in her throat. Turning from left to right she tried to see who had touched her.

"Stop this," she screamed. "Whoever it is, just stop it, just leave me alone." The silence mocked her. The only sound was the tick, tick, tick of the pipes as they cooled down.

Emma circled around once more, but no one was there, not even the cat. Had she imagined it? Was she going mad? Part of her wanted to leave, to grab her car keys and to just drive away from this awful house and to never come back. Only there was another part of her. This one needed to know what was going on, she needed to understand why this was happening. Somehow she knew that if she left that would be it. She would never lead an independent life again, and she could not bear that.

What she needed was to think this through and maybe to do a bit of research. There had to be a reason for these things happening and if she could find the reason then maybe she could... what... what was she thinking? Shaking her head in frustration, she walked towards the kitchen. As she passed beneath the banister something harsh pulled against her neck. It almost lifted her from her feet, cutting tight into her windpipe. Instinctively her hands reached up and sought to find what was holding her. As she struggled it pulled tighter and soon she could not breathe. Gasping, she fought with her arms, but nothing was there. There was nothing to grab hold of, nothing to pull away from, she scraped at her neck and could feel the skin coming away under her fingernails. Blood erupted between her fingers and her lungs burned as they desperately fought for oxygen. She tried to shout, tried to scream, tried to beg for mercy, but there was no room for any words to escape. The pain in her throat and the burning in her lungs was all she could think of. The air was frigid now, and yet the cold was a blessing. It calmed the burning in her neck calmed the burning in her lungs. Emma felt her eyes starting to close, felt as if she was falling into a deep pit and there would be no escaping.

As her eyes closed, the world started to blacken, and she could smell smoke, burning. Was this it? Was this the end? With her last breath, she reached up to try and pull the rope from her neck. She did not understand how she knew it was a rope, but she did. Not only was it a rope, but it was also a noose and whoever put it there intended to hang her. Circling her arms above her head, she flapped and fought like a crazy thing. Whatever energy she had left she would use to fight. Just as she thought it was too late, she felt herself lifted. As if her feet came off the floor and the pain in her neck was gone. The pressure eased. She drew in a gasping, shuddering breath and filled her grateful lungs with sweet, sweet air. The smoke was gone.

Dropping to her knees, she crawled into the kitchen and pulled herself into a chair. Though she wanted to run, she did not have the energy. So she collapsed down onto the table and gulped down great gasps of air until her head began to clear.

The house was quiet, calm, and the temperature was quite normal. Gradually she looked up, was she dreaming this? Was this all in her mind? Surely, it had to be for anything else was insanity. Looking down at her shaking hands she was dismayed to see the ends of her fingers and nails were covered in blood.

Emma stood, she desperately wanted to

wash the blood away and to look at her neck. The reflection in the window showed the claw marks that she had made to herself as well as a deep welt across her neck.

It was time to leave.

Her handbag and car keys were on the table, she turned back and as she did a shadow moved across her. Where it touched, she was instantly cold and yet, when she turned there was nothing there. Turning once more she saw the shadow in the window, it was in the shape of a man. His mouth was open in an agonizing scream. Emma grabbed her keys and turned towards the front door. Though she wanted to look back, she knew she must not. It was time to run, and she fled from the room as fast as her feet would carry her. Just before she got to the front door, a haze appeared before her. It was just a smudge on her vision, a little like seeing something out of the corner of your eye. Yet she knew it intended to stop her. To prevent her from leaving and the fear turned her knees to jelly.

"Let me go," she screamed. "Please, just let me go."

Whispers surrounded her, and yet she could not understand a thing. The noise grew like leaves in a storm, like waves rolling to a crescendo. Every now and then she could hear a word and the air filled with the scent of burning flesh.

"Go." Came clear between the static. "Death," the ghostly voice whispered. "Save."

Emma could not understand what they were saying, what it was saying to her, what did it want? She raised her hands to her ears trying to block out the noise, trying to shut it out but it would not work. The room started to spin, and she felt her vision darken. She knew she had to get out of there, that if she did not, then she would die. The room tilted and she started to stumble. Scrambling forward she reached for the door.

Emma collapsed onto the floor and was instantly unconscious, gradually, the murmuring stopped and the haze cleared from the room.

Chapter Eight

Emma awoke to the sound of a persistent meow. Opening her eyes, she saw the bright sunlight and winced. Where was she? What had happened? As the memory started to come back, she tried to sit up and felt a little dizzy. Then she heard the meow again, her head jerked to the sound. The awful black cat was sat staring at her, its amber eyes like two windows into hell. Jerking upright she scooted back on her bottom until she hit the door. The cat just stared, licking its lips, before walking away. Raising a shaking hand to her head, she tried to stop the pounding.

What had happened? With the sunlight

streaming in through the windows the house did not look scary. In fact, it just looked and smelled like something a little old lady would live in. Emma got to her feet and breathed in the scent of sage and lavender, she swallowed. Her throat was raw, and she needed a drink. Licking her lips and trying to form some saliva she knew she had to go to the kitchen.

The memory of the night before was fresh in her mind. What had she seen? In the daylight, it all seemed so silly. Maybe it was just a shadow, and yet she knew it was not. Something was wrong here, and she needed to find out what. Her handbag and coat were on the floor, her car keys were there too. Bending to pick them up she felt the blood rush to her head, and the pounding grew worse. A couple of paracetamol would go down well with a drink. She had to go to the kitchen.

Slowly she walked towards the kitchen. With each step closer her heart pounded faster and harder, what did she expect? *Nothing had happened during the day.* That thought strengthened her resolve, so she walked towards the kitchen. As she stepped around the door, she could see the cat, sat on the surface staring out the window. The tuna she had put down the night before was still there, untouched.

What sort of a cat was this?

Emma grabbed a glass and poured some water, then she found two paracetamol and swallowed them down with a few sips of water. As she swallowed her throat protested angrily and yet the water was soothing. Slowly, she sipped the rest of the glass. Placing it in the sink, she saw her fingers. They were still covered in blood. Turning on the tap, she scrubbed at them as hard and fast as she could. Tears dropped from her eyes as she watched the blood swirl away down the drain.

Emma left the house, climbed into the

Volvo and locked the doors. It had never felt so good to be inside the car. Everything about it was familiar, everything about it was real. Starting the engine, she drove away from the house. Once she was on the road, she pulled into a layby. Pulling down the visor she looked at her face in the mirror. She was pale, drawn. As she looked lower, she could see a red welt across her neck.

What had happened?

Then the tears began to fall. She leaned back into the seat and wept. It was real, something was wrong. Either that or she was so crazy that she had actually strangled herself.

***

Emma parked the car, grabbed her laptop, and went to the small cafe for her breakfast. She ordered a toasted teacake and a cappuccino and tried to stop the shaking while she waited for her order.

"Are you all right, my dear?" the waitress asked as she popped her order onto the table.

Emma swallowed, it was painful to speak. "Yes, thank you, just a bad night."

"If you need to talk, you can call me," the waitress said before walking away.

Emma smiled and felt a hysterical laugh bubbling up inside of her. The thought of telling somebody what had really happened was hilariously funny, and yet she had to tell someone.

She nibbled on the teacake and sipped at the cappuccino but she had no appetite, and the food was like burnt ash in her mouth. Leaving some money on the table, she left for the library.

Once in the library she opened up the laptop and logged onto the Internet. Her first thought was to Skype and to speak with Lynn.

Yet just as she was about to press the button her hand froze.

What could she say?

Even if Lynn believed her what could she do? Maybe she should just go back to London. Yet something was stopping her. When she was away from the house, it was as if she wanted to go back. As if there was unfinished business, as if there was something she had to do.

She sighed with exasperation... this was getting her nowhere.

Opening up a browser she typed in Brynlee House. There were no listings. So she typed in Brynlee. A definition came up.

An old English word meaning burnt clearing.

She remembered the smell from the house, how many times had it smelt like burnt ash? Suddenly, she felt excited. Maybe she could find something.

Yet, what should she type, what should she search for?

She pulled a notepad out of her bag and started writing down everything that had happened.

Cold spots.

Noises.

Screaming.

Child's laughter.

Dead cat moved.

Apparition.

The smell of burning.

Shudders ran down her spine as she remembered being in bed, somebody whispering into her ear.

She added whispering in the ear to the list.

Then in big letters, she wrote ghost and circled the word three times.

Did she really believe the house was haunted?

It didn't matter, she knew something was wrong, and she knew she had to find out what. So, she grabbed a coffee from the machine and sat back down. For the next two hours, she searched for all of the terms, along with the local area, along with Brynlee House. Bit by bit she uncovered a history. There was a rumor of a house called, 'the cage'. It had been used to torture and hang a local witch. The description of the house was vague, but the location sounded very much like where she was living. She read the article faster and faster, wanted to find out what was happening. Too soon she was finished, there was very little there. So she searched again and again. Now she had a name. The cage. Entering that alongside the word witch, she got three more results.

The first told of a witch who was killed there. Emma's blood ran cold as she read the name, Ursula Kemp. Her aunt's name was Sylvia Kemp. *Could this be a relative?*

She skipped to the next article, it didn't really tell her anything more so she went to the last one. Feeling a little sick she read the words quicker and quicker. A man named Alden Carter tortured the witch, Ursula Kemp, in the basement of the cage. It appeared he broke her by burning her daughter alive. Emma could feel tears prickling at the back of her eyes, and in her mind, she could hear the screaming of the child. Is that what she had been hearing?

She closed her eyes and thought back to the night before. Suddenly the words were clearer.

"Stop this."

The ghost wanted something. Did it want

her to stop what had happened? For that was not possible. Or did it want her to do something?

Emma knew she needed help and there was only one person she could ask. She finished her coffee, closed her laptop and left the library. The only problem she could see was he would think she was crazy. Maybe he would be right. Either she was crazy for thinking she saw ghosts, or she was crazy for trying to help them.

Chapter Nine

Emma walked the short distance to the police station trying to decide what she could say.

What would Brent think? Would he help?

She knew she had to handle this carefully, she could not just blurt out that the house was haunted. Yet, maybe she could say she thought someone had been there and ask him to come and look.

When she got to the station, there was a uniformed officer behind the counter.

"Can I help you miss?"

Emma had to swallow before she could get the words out. "Can I speak to Detective Inspector Brent Markham, please?"

The policeman smiled and indicated for her to take a seat. Within minutes Brent walked through the door and into the waiting area. There was a broad grin on his face, he seemed really pleased to see her. That was until he noticed the mark on her neck.

"What happened? Did he find you?"

Emma took a deep breath, how could she explain this. "It was last night. I got up for a drink and... I don't know who it was... Or what... I'm okay, though."

"Did you call 999?"

"My phone doesn't work there, and the landline has not been installed yet."

"I will sort something out about that. I think we should get you checked out by the doctor." Brent said as he sat down beside her.

"No, no, I'm all right... But I would like to ask a favor," Emma said and she was suddenly feeling excited. Before she could analyze the feelings, he answered.

"Anything."

"Would you come back to the house with me? Would you have another look around? Maybe cut down those branches and just check that there is no one there?"

"My shift finishes in half an hour." he said and looked over at the counter. "Heck, this is work, let's go now. Just give me a moment."

Brent walked towards the counter where he spoke to the officer behind it for a few minutes. Taking something from the man, he returned to her.

"I want you to take this. It's a police radio. I told them you're having problems with an intruder. I don't want you to stay in that house... but just in case you do, or wherever you are, if you get into trouble you use this radio. I'm off shift now, but I will have my radio on all night. If you need me, I will be there. I want you to call no matter what. If you hear anything, see anything, even think someone is there, call me, and I will be there."

Emma took the radio and nodded. "Thank you," she said as she wiped tears away from her eyes.

Brent held out his arm and gave her a big smile. "Okay, Emma? Let's go see what we can find."

Emma looked at his arm and the smile on his face and felt herself blush. Did he think? "This is not a date," she said. "I'm just desperate, I need your help. You must understand this is not a date."

Brent flashed a large injured smile. "That's

the story of my life, no woman will have me unless she is desperate."

Emma could not help but laugh.

***

This time Brent drove first and Emma followed him back to the house. It was still daylight, and the place looked a little spooky. Yet, much of what she thought, much of what she had read suddenly seemed so foolish. Then she swallowed, and her injured throat reminded her just how real it really was.

Brent opened her car door and bowed to let her out. Emma found herself laughing again and yet the old fear was still there. It was wrong to trust a man, any man. That way only led to pain.

"Come on, let's go inside," Brent said. "Then I want you to stay in the kitchen while I search through the house."

Emma nodded and followed him as he approached the house. It was always cold under the trees, and she shivered slightly as they walked down the moss covered path. When they reached the house, she looked at the sign. It was still askew and didn't look quite right. She reached out to touch it, and as she did, it moved beneath her fingers. Taking hold with both hands, she pulled it up until eventually, it came off the wall. Underneath was a stone. Carved into it were two words.

The Cage.

Chapter Ten

Brent guided her into the house, he could see that she was shaken up and he understood. Something about the house had disturbed her, and he felt it too, he wanted to know what it was. As she sat down at the table and he put on the kettle, he decided he was going to do something. He was going to research the house, and he would find out what the problem was. His logical mind revolted against this, but maybe somebody had been here before. It was strange that he didn't like this place, that it gave him the creeps, but somehow, he knew that something about it was not right

"You drink this coffee, I made it nice and

strong. I'm gonna have a quick look around in here, outside, and then check upstairs. You just stay here and relax."

"I can't do that," Emma said. "I just feel stupid, I think this is all stress."

Brent dropped to his knees and took her hand in his. "Maybe it is, but I'm the detective here, right? Let me have a look around and see what I can detect."

Emma nodded and took a sip of coffee. She winced, boy he was right, it was strong.

Brent looked around the kitchen. There was very little to see. A few cupboards, an old dresser, and the door leading to the outside. He took his time and realized he didn't want to leave her alone. Maybe it was stress. That would be what his boss would tell him. Yet, his instincts told him something different. There was definitely something wrong with this place.

The only other thing in the kitchen was the door outside to the porch. He turned the handle, and it was locked. As he did, he heard a faint, high-pitched sound and felt cold air blast across the back of his neck. Instinctively he turned around, there was nothing there, just a strange shadow on the white wall behind him. It coalesced, marring the white paint and it made him feel queasy. Then it was gone, it must have been his own shadow, somehow the light must have cast it on the wall. Yet, where had the draft come from? Logic said it couldn't come from the door that was in front of him but there was nothing behind him. Just a solid wall. Maybe this house was getting to him too.

"I'm gonna take a look around the rest of the house," he said.

Emma was watching him, and he wanted to see her smile. Her lips twitched, that was enough, it was a start. "When I'm finished I'll come down and cut off those branches. Do you have any tools?"

Emma shook her head.

"No worries, I'm sure I can find something in my car. Now, I'm gonna look around, check for signs of entry. I won't be a moment, you shout if you need me."

Emma nodded again, and he was sure he saw another faint glimpse of a smile. That made all this worthwhile.

***

Emma watched Brent as he looked around the kitchen. She was not sure what he was expecting to find but felt comforted with him being here. Yet he also made her nervous. Part of her wanted to sit down with him and talk and laugh and joke just like normal people.

Part of her wanted to tell him to go, to leave and to never come back. The old fear was heavy on her chest, and she was struggling to cope with it. Yet she did not want to be alone in this house, not until she was sure that she was safe.

As Brent looked around the kitchen, she was sure he had seen something. Maybe it was the shadow, the stain on the wall that she had seen before? Maybe he had felt the draft, but then he just turned back to the door as if nothing has happened. Was this all in her mind?

She could hear Brent walking around the lower level of the house. He was knocking on walls, opening doors, and moving furniture. Suddenly, she felt so silly, what was she expecting him to find? Did she think that Mark was here, hidden behind the sofa just waiting to pop out at her whenever she fell asleep? Maybe she did, maybe that's what her subconscious felt. Maybe that was why she heard all the strange things. Yet it didn't explain the injury to her neck or the cat... what could explain those two?

Brent had gone upstairs and again she could hear him walking around and suddenly, she felt very alone. The wind whistled through the trees whispering to her and the branches scratched against the window. The pitch changed, it sounded just like a scream and then the wind dropped, and it sounded like laughter. The light and joyous laughter of a child. It looked like she really was going crazy... like this was all in her mind.

Brent came back into the room. "I've had a good look around, and I can't see anything out of order."

"Maybe it's all in my mind," she said, her eyes beseeching him to deny her.

Brent crossed the room and put a hand on her shoulder. Emma jerked backward almost knocking her chair over. In her chest, her heart was pounding, and her throat was as dry as sawdust. "I'm sorry," she said "I'm so sorry... I just... I just... I'm not ready, not yet."

Brent pulled his hand back and looked down at her so calmly that it relieved her nerves. "I understand," he said. "I'm happy to just be here as a friend, to help you out. I'm going to leave you that radio and tonight, no matter what happens, if you need somebody, anybody, you call me. There is no pressure, I don't want anything from you. I just want you to feel safe."

Emma felt tears pricking at the back of her eyes. She nodded. "Thank you."

"Now, let's chop down those trees. I'll just nip to the car, I have a knife in there."

"There's an axe in the shed if that's any good?" Emma said, remembering the wood and the axe she had seen there.

"That will do even better," Brent said and gave her a 'Here's Johnny' grin.

Emma couldn't help but laugh, and suddenly all the tension was gone.

Brent reached for the key in the door. As he did, the sound of a child's scream filled the room. Emma felt her heart start to pound, her palms were sweating, she wanted to run. Only she saw the look on Brent's face and realized he had heard it too. She wasn't going mad. He had heard it, but had it been a child's scream?

"Stay here," Brent said, and he went out the door.

Suddenly, she was alone, and the fear was like a physical force weighing her down and she could not take it. She had to follow him, would not be alone in this house again. Yet, she had been sure the scream had come from behind her, from the wall with the disappearing stain. Brent had looked the other way, he must have heard it in front of him.

The scream came again, louder this time and definitely in front of her. Emma feared for Brent, and she ran out the door, only to find him laughing. "What the... What the heck is going on? she asked.

Brent moved the branches across the window. As he did she heard the sound of the scream, it was exactly as she had heard just a moment ago. He stopped, the scream stopped, he moved the branch again, slower this time. The sound of a child's laughter filled the air.

"This can't be real," she said. "How can a tree sound so... so eerily like a child?"

"I don't know, but I promise you I will not be putting in my report quite how scared that sound made me."

"My big, brave detective," Emma said laughing and then blushed furiously as she realized what she had just said.

Brent just laughed. Taking the axe, he began to hack away at the branches and soon they were all chopped down. He had found a few larger ones. When they hit the house, it sounded just like knocking. It looked like half of the things she imagined were just the trees. Emma felt the tension release, she stood back and watched him work. It was strangely satisfying and nice to see him doing this, just for her. As she moved, the soil beneath her felt strange to her feet, almost silky. She looked down to see that she was standing in a circle of burnt ground. *'Brynlee – Burnt Clearing.'* It looked like it had been burnt recently and she felt the breath catch in her throat.

"What is this?" she asked.

Brent had finished chopping, he put down the axe and wiped the sweat from his brow. Then he walked over and looked at the ground. Dropping to his knees, he ran his fingers through the ash. "Looks like somebody set a fire here recently, I guess you have had intruders. Maybe you shouldn't stay here because they could come back."

Intruders.

So somebody had been here, maybe somebody had attacked her. Could that explain what had happened to her neck? It seemed as if everything had been explained and it was all totally logical.

"I think they've gone now. I feel safer."

"Then why don't you make me another coffee?" Brent said. "We can talk. I will stay here as long as you want."

Emma blushed and nodded at the house indicating for them to go back inside.

This time she made the coffee while Brent sat at the table. He talked about the local town, about his job, about the weather. About anything just to make her feel better, and it did.

Emma put two mugs of coffee on the table and sat down opposite him. "I can't thank you enough for coming. With your great detective skills, it looks like everything has been explained."

"Everything except your neck," he said. "You never told me what happened."

Emma didn't quite know what to say. She had explained about cold spots, about everything, but how could she explain that this injury appeared to be from a cobweb?

"I won't judge you, Emma."

"I know... it is just that it was so strange."

Brent reached across and took her hand, this time she did not pull back. It felt nice, comforting, and yet there really was no pressure.

Nothing was said for a few seconds, but it was not uncomfortable. Emma knew she had to tell him, she just needed to find a way to do it. As she opened her mouth to speak the temperature in the room dropped 20°. Her breath frosted before her face.

Brent's eyes widened, he had seen it.

"Did you see that?" she asked.

He nodded.

"So many times in this room I have felt a chill, a draft, or it has been so cold that I have seen my own breath. That just doesn't seem normal."

"I felt a draft too," he said. "I thought I saw something on that wall."

Emma knew her eyes were wide with surprise, he had seen something.

"Tell me what happened to your neck and

then we will investigate this cold."

Emma let out a big sigh, maybe it was just best to tell him. "It has happened a few times now, only the last time was by far the worst. I feel a presence, a malevolence, the room goes cold, it smells of burning. I came across the hallway, it is always directly beneath the banister, something touches my face. I think it's a cobweb, my arms fly out in panic. I know it's stupid, but I hate spiders. Then, whatever it is... it gets coarser, stronger. The last time it came across my throat I felt it lift me from my feet and I could not breathe. I thought I was going to die. Then I felt a different presence, and suddenly I was free. I know what you think... that I'm going crazy, and maybe you're right."

"No, I don't think that," Brent said. "Maybe there had been an intruder? It was dark and late, and the mind can play tricks on you. I will get to the bottom of this for you. I promise."

Emma nodded and smiled. Right then she wished she could lay her head against his chest and just let him put his arms around her. The fact that she could even think such a thing shocked her to her core.

Suddenly, the room was cold again. Both Brent and Emma's breath misted in the air before them. The air filled with smoke, it made them cough and choke and yet they could see nothing. Emma felt an oppressive weight on her chest, it was as if the room was pressing against her and it felt like evil.

Caroline Clark

Chapter Eleven

Emma tried to talk, but her voice was trapped in her throat. Fear had formed a lump there and would not allow the words to escape.

Brent had not noticed her reaction, he stood, and slowly he looked around the room. It was as if he was searching for someone. He coughed as if he smelt the smoke.

"You feel it too," Emma said. "You feel the presence, and it is evil."

Brent looked at her, and for a moment she thought he was going to agree.

Instead, he shook his head. "There has to be a logical explanation, there just has to be."

The air seemed to clear, and the room was warmer again, even if only a little bit.

It was as if the words gave him strength. He approached the wall. As he touched it, Emma saw it turn black beneath his fingers and yet he did not blink. It was obvious all he saw was the wall. Emma wanted to tell him to move, that it was evil, and that they should just leave. Yet he ran his hands across the wall. Reaching up towards the ceiling. Tapping, moving his hand, tapping again, and again. To her, his fingers were sinking into the mold, and it made her want to gag. Yet he just kept tapping on different parts of the wall. Then she heard it. A different sound on one part of the wall. It was hollow.

"You heard the difference didn't you?" Brent asked.

Emma nodded though she did not know what it meant.

Brent was tapping along the wall, pushing and shoving and searching with his fingers. He squatted down onto the floor and ran his hands along the skirting board. Then he looked at her, and a smile came over his face.

What had he found?

She watched as he pressed a mark on the skirting board. There was a groan and a scraping sound and then the sound of ripping plaster. As she watched, the wall started to crumble in places. Chunks of plaster dropped to the floor, and a door-shaped section of the wall swung away from them. In its place was a dark cavernous void that filled her with dread.

Brent turned to her and smiled. It appeared that he was happy with the discovery and yet the black hole before them scared the living daylights out of her.

"This explains the draft," Brent said.

Emma could not help but think he looked like an excited child. Like one about to go on an adventure. Yet she hoped that he would pull the door closed, bolt it and seal it off so that they could never even know that it had been there.

"You have a flashlight?" he asked.

Emma shook her head. Even if she had she would not have found it, would not have made it easier for him to go into that evil void.

"I have one in the car. Just give me a minute, and we can see what is down there."

Brent was gone before she could say a thing. He left her alone in the cold kitchen with that awful empty hole. Emma wanted to run after him, but her legs would not hold her. She forced a deep breath into her lungs and tried to calm the panic. Nothing had happened. It was just another room, and maybe he was right, maybe this was the cause of all the cold.

A low groan came out of the entrance. Emma felt the hair rising on her arms, and she could not breathe. Then she heard something behind her, a meow. Looking down she saw the cat. Its amber eyes found hers and seemed to challenge her as it strolled into the room. She hadn't seen the cat for some time. It was strange, for when it was not there she forgot all about it. Now it was here again, and just the sight of it made her skin crawl and her stomach roll. She could almost feel the sawdust beneath its fur. The weight and feeling of a stuffed shape and yet here it was walking, stalking, and challenging her with its eyes. It made no sense, and for a moment she wanted to scream. Just as she opened her mouth, Brent walked back into the kitchen. The look on his face was one of pure excitement, of discovery. Somehow having him back made everything seem less real. He was right, it was just another room, and she was just letting her imagination get the better of her.

Yet, if it was just another room then why had it been hidden behind a wall?

"Are you ready?" Brent asked.

Emma wanted to say no, she wanted to say there was no way she was going down there. And yet she found her head nodding.

Brent nodded and turned on the flashlight. He shone it into the hole. The beam cut through only a few feet of darkness. They could see a narrow staircase leading down into the gloom. The last thing Emma wanted to do was go down there, and yet she knew she would.

"It's dark, be careful on the stairs," Brent said as he stepped into the dark.

Emma hesitated for a moment. She could feel something down there, something evil. As she stood on the threshold, she felt the caress of a breath on her ear. It was just the tiniest of touches, just a brush of air, and yet it froze her to the spot. Something was whispering to her, but she could not hear it over the pounding of her heart. She tried to listen yet at the same time tried to run, but her legs would not move.

"You can stop this," the voice said.

"Who is this? Emma asked. "Leave me alone."

"You will die." This voice was in her other ear, and it sounded like a man. An angry man.

Emma put her hands over her head trying to shut out the voices, but she could not shut out the feeling of somebody there. At last, her legs would move, and she rushed towards the opening. She could see Brent halfway down the stairs. It could have only been a moment or two since he stepped into the void and yet it felt like she had been hearing voices for several minutes.

What was wrong with her?

As she got closer to Brent, the feeling of oppression left her, and she felt as if they were alone again.

"This place is amazing, don't you think?" Brent asked.

Emma nodded but amazing was not the thought she was having.

"Take your time," he said. "Just take one step at a time and keep close to me."

Emma could do that. The last place she wanted to be was down here, but if she was going to be, then she would definitely stay close to Brent.

They reached the bottom, and he shone the torch around the room. It looked like it extended the whole length of the house and yet the torch beam barely pierced the darkness. Cobwebs clung to their faces, and Emma felt her arms fly to her face in panic.

Brent moved away from her going to the closest wall on the left. Gradually, he started to walk around the room. It smelt of damp, it was cold, but nowhere nearly as cold as the draft they had felt earlier. The floor was made of dust, cobwebs were everywhere, and yet it just seemed like an empty room. Still, Emma wanted out of there. If she stayed in this house, she wanted it filled with concrete and maybe blessed by a priest.

"There's something over here," Brent said.

Emma followed him as quickly as she could across the dusty floor. There in the corner, she saw her worst nightmare. There were heavy iron shackles on the walls, the brickwork appeared to be stained, and all she could think of was that it was the blood of her ancestors. A metal cage stood empty next to the wall. This was it, this was the place she had read about. It was a place of torture and death, and it was why the house was haunted.

Haunted, had she really thought that?

Only now that she had, it made sense. Ursula Kemp, her ancestor, had been murdered here, so had her daughter. That was the worst thing that could happen to a parent. To know that your child was killed unlawfully. It made sense that it would be enough to turn someone into an evil spirit. Did she believe in this now? In spirits? It explained everything. The laughing child was Ursula's daughter. Laughing one moment and screaming the next. And yet Brent had proven that it was just a branch.

All of a sudden Brent let out a burst of laughter.

Emma looked at him and tried to work out why.

"Don't you understand?" he said. "It's a dungeon."

"Why is that funny? I think my family were

tortured down here and killed," she said.

Brent laughed again and reached out a hand to take hers. "I'm a detective, remember. I've seen a few things in my life, and this room was not meant for torture... well, not the kind that kills people anyway. It's a dungeon, a play dungeon, a sexual dungeon."

Emma felt heat hit her cheeks, could she be so naïve? Was he right, was this a place of pleasure or was it the place of torture and death.

Somehow she thought the latter, but maybe that was just her nerves and stress once more. "You might be right, but this place really creeps me out. Can we get out of here?"

Brent nodded and led her back to the stairs.

Caroline Clark

Chapter Twelve

Brent stayed for another hour. They talked and even laughed a little. Before he left, he found some screws and wood and fastened up the door to the dungeon. It made her feel slightly better, but only slightly. Now she knew it was there and despite everything they had said she felt it was a place of evil.

Brent had suggested she go and stay in a hotel or that he would stay with her. For some reason, she had said no. Yet now he was gone, she wished with all her heart that she had gone with him or let him stay.

Fatigue weighed heavily on her, she was so tired she did not think she could make the drive back into Castleton. So, she went up to the bedroom, only to find the cat lying on her bed. Tears sprang instantly to her eyes. She wanted to throw it off, to chase it from the room, but after all, it was only a cat. So, instead she climbed into the bed in her clothes and tried not to let it touch her.

Emma had expected it to take ages to fall asleep, and yet her head had barely touched the pillow before she was gone. It was some hours later when she felt a presence in the room. The sound of voices drifted into her subconscious, and she felt something touching her ear.

"You have to stop this," the voice hissed.

Emma rolled in her sleep but did not wake. As her legs moved, she touched the cat. It was just a solid lump, there was no give, no muscle, no sinew, and no life. Emma was jerked instantly awake.

Her heart pounded as she lay in the bed trying to work out what had awoken her. Then she heard it again, barely audible whispers, they were so close the person had to be on the bed with her. Emma let out a scream and scooted back up the bed. She had left the hall light on, and she could see shapes, but there was nothing solid. It was as if a dark mist formed and then separated and then formed again. It was in the shape of two people that became one. Were they fighting? Hugging? Blinking her eyes, she tried to focus, and she felt the touch of breath against her ear.

This was too much, she could not cope.

Leaping from the bed, she grabbed the radio and ran to the stairs. As she reached the hallway, she could see the shape of a noose hanging down before her. Pressing the button on the radio, she heard nothing but static. "Brent," she shouted, but the radio simply hissed at her. "Brent... anyone, please help me."

The radio hissed in the still house, and before her, the noose swung creating crazy big shadows across the wall and floor. It was in the exact place where she had hurt her neck, the place where something had touched her time and time again. Ice water ran through her veins and seemed to stop her heart. Turning away from the noose she ran to the front door. Stopping quickly to avoid tripping over the cat.

It stood before her, its eyes like fiery pits, its back arched and teeth drawn back. "Get away from me," she yelled, and for a moment it stayed there.

"Don't go," a voice whispered in her ear and yet it did not seem threatening. For a moment it lulled her and made her want to stay. The sound was familiar and warming. She shook her head to clear the thoughts.

"DON'T GO," a deeper voice yelled, commanded and this one scared her witless.

Emma grabbed her car keys and jumped over the cat. She fiddled with the door, almost dropping the keys. Then the lock turned, and she pulled the door. It slammed away from her hands. She pulled again, and this time it was as if she had help.

"Come back to us," the whisper said, and she could swear she felt lips moving against her ear.

Emma ran, she was out of the house, her feet carrying her away from it as fast as they could. She ran across the yard, down the mossy path, through the trees, and to the car. Pressing the button, she watched the lights flash, and she was in the door, pulling it closed behind her and pressing the button again to lock the doors tight. A gasp escaped her, and hot tears flowed down her face. Somehow, she never expected to be allowed to leave, and yet here she was in the car. She felt the radio in her hand. Would it work now? Should she call Brent?

She wanted to more than anything, she

wanted him here and yet? She pressed the button on the radio, the static had gone. Quickly, she checked her mobile, she had a signal, it was faint but there.

Glancing at her watch, she could see it was 3 AM. Soon it would be light, she was away from the house and safe. She could simply sleep in the car, she would be safe, and then drive into town once it was light.

Chapter Thirteen

Somehow, knowing that her mobile was working gave Emma the peace she needed to sleep. She reclined the car seat back and closed her eyes. She did not expect sleep to come and yet within minutes exhaustion had claimed her and taken her down to sweet oblivion.

She was woken by the notification of her phone receiving a text. It was light out, and she rubbed her eyes as she came awake. For a moment, she was confused, where was she? What happened? Then it all came back. The voices? The feeling of both familiarity and fear? The darned cat stopping her at the door. She had to get away from this house and yet for some reason, she felt drawn back to it. Taking a breath, she reached across to check her phone.

The fact that it had worked filled her with a sense of safety. Maybe it was Lynn... that would certainly cheer her up.

As she looked at the text, she froze. It was a number she recognized, it was Mark. How had he found her new number!? Did he know where she was? Suddenly, everything in the house made sense, it had to be Mark. Playing jokes on her. What else could it be? He was simply trying to scare her back to London. Emma was engulfed by fear and exhaustion, and she wanted to give in. To run back to the shelter where Mark could never enter. What should she do? She thought of Lynn, of her friends and the work they had put in. How they told her she must stand firm and never let him beat her. That was what she would do. He would not scare her. It would not work this time, she would not let him rule her life.

Emma heard the sound of a vehicle, and her heart missed a beat.

Was he here?

She looked around to see a car pulling up behind her. A huge wave of relief washed over her as she realized it was Brent. Part of her was so relieved to see him and yet another part was once again scared of men. As he came up to the door, she could see the look of confusion on his face. What should she say?

"Did you sleep in the car?" he asked.

Emma laughed and ran a hand through her hair. She knew it must certainly look as if she slept in the car but she did not want him to know that. "I came out to use my phone." She shrugged her shoulders after getting out of the car in her night clothes. Looking down she realized she was barefoot and dirty. Her hands were shaking, but she hoped he did not notice.

"Emma, please tell me what's wrong," Brent said. "Did something happen last night?"

How could she explain what happened? When it must all be in her mind. Instead, she handed him the phone. The text was still there unopened, unread. She did not know if she had the courage to look at it.

"Is this from the ex?" Brent asked.

Emma nodded.

Brent took the phone and led the way back to the house. The door was standing open, he walked in and went straight to the kitchen, putting on the kettle.

"Take a seat," he said and sat down to face her. Then he looked at the phone, opened the text, and read it. "He hasn't found you," Brent said. "He has your phone number, which is bad, but not the end of the world. We change your phone today. From now on I will be here at night just to make sure that you are okay. That he doesn't find you."

"What does it say?" Emma asked even though she didn't really want to hear.

Brent got up to make the coffee. "It's just the normal type of bullying," he said as he put two mugs on the table.

"I think it must have been him all along?" Emma said. "All these things I've been seeing, they weren't real, they were just in my mind. They were just Mark messing with me."

"I saw some things too," Brent said.

Emma shook her head, she knew she had imagined things, and the last thing she wanted was to be humored. It was time to face up to it, she was suffering from stress.

After two rounds of toast and copious amounts of coffee, Brent took her phone, promising to bring her a new one that night. Gently, he reached out and held her hand. Emma pulled back, and she could see the look of hurt in his eyes.

"I'm sorry," she said.

"Don't worry, I will be back tonight." Finally, he left to go to work.

Once the house was empty again, Emma felt afraid. What if Mark had found her? What if he was here hiding?

In the end, the solitude and quietness of the house were too much. Emma had a quick shower, got dressed, grabbed her laptop and drove into Castleton.

At least there she could Skype with Lynn and tell her what had happened.

***

Sat in the café with a toasted teacake and hot chocolate, Emma Skyped Lynn. It was so good to see her friend's face and they spent the first few minutes just catching up.

"I can see something's wrong," Lynn said at last.

"Am I so obvious?" Emma shrugged her shoulders, but she knew that she looked terrible.

Lynn laughed. "Yes, I guess you are, now come on, tell me what the problem is."

So Emma told her everything. All the problems she had with the house. The injury to her neck. The secret room, the screaming, the weird cat that didn't seem to be alive and yet was. Then she told her about the whispering, the feeling of somebody touching her ear and talking to her. How sometimes she felt that she was wanted there, that she had to be there.

Yet sometimes she felt she was in danger. When she had gone through all of this, then she told Lynn about the text.

"So you've heard everything, do you think

it is all stress, do you think this is just Mark?"

Emma could see Lynn thinking. For once she was not laughing and bubbly and making light of what had happened. That in itself was worrying.

"This policeman doesn't think that Mark is there?" Lynn said.

"No, he doesn't, but what else could it be?"

"Maybe you should come back," Lynn said.

For some reason, the thought of going back to London, of leaving the house filled Emma with fear. Was it because Mark was in London? Maybe he wasn't, maybe he was here. Somehow the thought of leaving the house left her feeling empty and yet the thought of staying terrified her.

How could she sort out a problem like that? So, she tried to explain that to Lynn. That she felt as if she had to stay and yet she felt as if she would be in danger if she stayed.

"You know what we usually do in this sort of problem," Lynn said and then laughed. "Okay, maybe we don't get many of this sort of problem. But the technique would still work. Go back to the library and research that house. Find out everything you can about it. Then write it down, everything, including what you feel. Just let the words come, let them flow, let everything out about how you feel.

Then read it all back until you understand how it makes you feel. Keep writing and reading until you understand what you want to do... and then, do what we always do, take it outside and burn it."

Emma knew this was a good idea and just listening to it made her feel excited, and yet when Lynn said burn it, all she could think of was the burnt ground outside the house and the smell of smoke, of burning that sometimes filled the house.

Chapter Fourteen

Emma went to the library and tried to research the house. The only problem was she couldn't find out anything more than she already knew and she was becoming more and more frustrated. She was searching around the back of the bookshelves, looking for anything, when a hand touched her shoulder. She jumped into the air and let out a shriek, only to turn around and see Janet stood there, a startled expression on her face.

"Sorry," Janet said. "Are you looking for anything in particular?"

Emma ran a hand through her hair and tried to talk. It was difficult because she was still feeling shaky. Now she even felt embarrassed, about leaping into the air, shrieking, and because she was looking into whether her house was haunted or not. Then she remembered that Janet had actually hinted at such things. Maybe she could help. "I wanted to find out more about the house," she said.

Janet's face seemed to light up. "I know of a couple of books, they are very old and difficult to read, but I think they are what you are looking for." Without waiting for an answer, Janet walked through the book shelves further and further away from the desk until stopping in the very corner. Dropping to her knees, she started searching through the books.

"It looks like only one of them is here," she said. "I can't understand who would have the other one, but I will ask Judy at the desk."

Emma nodded and together they took the book over to a table. The book was a fascinating, if scary reading. It told of witch trials that took place in the town, and it didn't take long for her to find a mention of a building called The Cage. There was a pencil drawing of the property, and it was obvious that it was her house. A shudder ran down her spine as she read on about it. The book told of the torture that had taken place there. Finally, she read about a woman called Ursula Kent who was the last person to be tortured there. The book told of how the Inquisitor found it impossible to break Ursula. How she denied everything despite the fact that he tortured her. Emma felt a lump in her throat and tears in her eyes as she continued reading.

A man named Alden Carter had taken Ursula's daughter and burned her alive just outside the back door of the house. A shudder ran down Emma's spine. Just outside the back door of the house! That was exactly where she had found a burnt circle. No, this was ridiculous, this book was written in the 1700's. There was no way the ground would still be burned... that there would still be ash there.

She read on and found her hand was shaking. Ursula's black cat, Gaia, was also burned outside of the house, and his bones, along with those of the child, were thrown into the cellar. The book said that the creature's spirit still resided there.

Emma slammed the book closed. *This was ridiculous.* How could she even think that the two cats could be the same? And yet somehow. she knew they were.

"You have seen things, haven't you?" Janet said.

Emma had actually forgotten she was still there and she looked up, surprised.

What should I say?

Should she confide in this woman and be seen as someone who was losing her mind?

"I understand," Janet said. "You don't want to admit anything. I've seen things too, and I know what you are going through. The other book tells you more, it tells you things you need to know. Until you have read it, you must not go back in that house. It has never been easy for your family, no one has been happy there and may have died too young."

Emma could feel her heart pounding. What should she do?

"You need the manuscript, it will tell you more." Janet was looking concerned. "Let's ask the librarian if it's been moved somewhere."

Emma nodded. She had read everything from this book, and though chilled to the bone, there was nothing more to learn from it. So she followed Janet to the librarian's desk, and they asked about the other book.

Judy looked a little shocked for a moment.

What now? Emma thought.

"Oh, how very strange," Judy said. "That nice Detective Markham borrowed that very same item this morning."

Emma felt her blood run cold. Did Brent know something? Was he trying to hide something from her? She knew she would have to ask him, and yet somehow she dreaded doing so.

***

After Janet left, Emma retired to a far corner of the library and tried to gather her thoughts. She was torn between thinking that she had lost her mind. That she had succumbed to the stress of the move or the possibility that Mark had found her, or that something strange was going on in the house. Taking out a pad and pencil she wrote down all these thoughts. Was she losing her mind? Her hand rose to her neck, and she could feel the damage there.

Something had grazed the skin and left a deep welt. Could she really believe that she had done that to herself? If she hadn't done it then was it an intruder? That didn't make sense. No one was there... but surely, they had to be... and yet, after the incident, all she had found was a cobweb. There was no way that a cobweb could have torn her skin and cut off her breath! It just wasn't possible. So that left only one explanation, something was wrong in the house. Something was going on.

Could it really be haunted?

Emma did not believe in such things. Yes, evil existed in the world, but it was human and mean. She put down the pen and stared at the notes she had made. Here in the peaceful library, feeling safe and with the sun shining in through the window it all seemed so stupid. Yet, when the darkness fell, she knew she would be afraid.

What should I do?

Closing her eyes, she did what she had been taught at the center. She let go of everything and cleared her mind. Then she let her heart tell her what she must do. Should she leave and go back to London? After asking the question, she sat quietly and waited. The answer she received was not the one she wanted.

Chapter Fifteen

Emma drove back to the house. She knew she should be afraid. Either she was losing her mind, or she was about to face a ghost. A relative and her daughter were murdered there. One inside and one outside the house. That sort of blood would leave a stain on anything.

How could anyone murder a child, burn it alive just to torture the mother? Every time she thought about it, Emma just felt sick. The pain Ursula must've felt was unimaginable, and poor little Rose. No child deserved to die in such pain, to feel such fear.

How could she ever ease the pain that tainted this house?

While she was at the library, Emma had done some more research. At the time it seemed sensible, that she would arm herself against the spirits. Yet, as she approached the house it seemed childish, stupid, but it was all that she had.

As she walked into the house, the cat was sat beneath the banister. Its amber eyes glared at her, and it sat in the exact place she had seen the noose, where she had felt the noose. Where she had almost been hung!

"Gaia," Emma said feeling rather silly.

The cat's ears pricked up and its eyes seemed to mellow. It was as if the fire inside of them began to fade.

"So, Gaia, show me what I need to know," Emma said.

Gaia looked at her and then turned to walk away. Skirting around the bottom of the banister she followed the cat to the kitchen. It stopped in front of a cupboard, jumped onto the surface and rubbed itself against the door. Emma opened the cupboard, and she understood. She pulled the salt out of the cupboard and placed it on the surface. Gaia walked across to the window, to the sage plant that grew there. He meowed in front of it and touched the bell. Emma grabbed some scissors, cut off some of the sage and placed it in her pocket. Then the cat walked to the wall and disappeared through it.

Emma's breath caught in her throat, and she gasped. For a moment she could not move, but somehow she knew that time was short. That if she was to survive this, then she must act quickly. She went to the back door, opened it, and stepped out into the garden. The sun was going down, and it was already feeling gloomy. The light seemed to shine on the circle, the burnt circle. Then Emma remembered the first time she had looked into the house. The name Brynlee. It meant burnt clearing. Was this a clue? Had her relatives named the house to give her a clue? Or had they done it to simply torment themselves? The cat pawed at the ash. Emma bent down and ran her fingers through it. It was as cold as ice and yet felt silky against the skin.

What am I supposed to do here?

The trees began to whisper, the leaves mumbling and chattering softly at first and yet the sound grew. It rose as if the wind was blowing a gale and yet the night was still. Soon the leaves tossed and the branches rubbed together, grating, murmuring, now they sounded like an angry mob.

"What do you want? Emma shouted. "What do you want from me?"

The noise stopped and was replaced with a deathly silence.

Unsure what else to do Emma took some sage from her pocket and scattered it over the ashes. As she did, the cat stood and walked back towards the house. The wind whistled behind Emma, and the shadows seemed to lengthen. It was getting colder, and a feeling of menace, of oppression, surrounded her. As she watched, the cat disappeared through the door. Emma knew she must follow and yet suddenly, the house felt dangerous.

As she stood, she felt a hand grasp onto her wrists. It was cold, frigid and so tight it seemed to bruise her bones.

Jerking violently she pulled her hand free and spun around, but there was no one there.

It was time to leave. What did she think she was doing here?

Emma almost ran back to the house. As she pushed through the door, she saw a presence before her. The air coalesced and swirled and seemed to form the shape of a translucent woman dressed in white. Her arms reached out to Emma's, beseeching her. Then the figure turned to mist, and the mist rushed towards Emma. She tried to move, but her legs would not hold her. She was engulfed in cold and felt the touch of lips against her ear.

"End thissss," the voice said.

Emma's hands flapped like a child's in the eye of a nightmare. Yet, she could not feel anything, there was nothing to fight, there was nothing to stop. It seemed that she was at the spirit's mercy.

Every fiber of her being wanted to leave. She wanted to grab her bag and run from the house, never to return, and yet she knew she could not. Somehow, she had to help this woman. The presence had shocked her, scared her, and yet, it did not feel threatening. It did not want to hurt her. It wanted her help. Though she did not know why, that was what she felt. What she could do?

The door slammed behind her. Emma jumped. "Shit!" she shouted and turned to face the door.

There was something there, something dark, something insubstantial and yet it had slammed the door. A darkness cleaved out of the air to become almost a man. Then the figure turned into mist. Swarming like angry bees, it seemed to buzz around her, and she felt the hair on her arms raise. Heart pounding, her breath caught in her throat, and she was weighed down with a deep sense of dread and danger. Was this what grabbed her?

Slowly, she backed away from the presence. As she did, Gaia rushed past her and dived at the shadow. As he hit it, it dissipated and was gone.

Emma let out a sob and collapsed to her knees. How much more could she cope with?

Emma got to her feet, there was nothing there. The cat had also disappeared, and yet, Emma heard a meow behind her. Turning, she saw the cat sat before her at the door to the dungeon. To the cage. The door was open. All the boards that Brent had put over it were gone. There was just a dark, gaping hole, and it was waiting for her.

Emma knew she had to go down there, though she did not know why.

Taking a deep breath, she stepped towards the opening. There was light at the bottom. It was faint, enough for her to see the lower steps but nothing more. Gaia turned, meowed, and then trotted onto the stairs. As she watched, the cat faded into the darkness. Emma knew she had to follow.

***

Emma pulled her phone out of her pocket and activated the torch app. The last thing she wanted to do was go down into the dark and yet she knew she must. Taking a deep breath, she put one foot on the stairs. They creaked beneath her as if they would not support her weight. Still, she had to go down, and so she took another step. Cobwebs tickled her hands, and one thin filament drifted across her face. This time it did not faze her, there was worse to come, of that she was sure. So, she took another step and then another until she had walked down the steps one by one. With each step, her heart beat faster and the breath caught in her throat. Strange shadows flicked across the walls as she approached the flickering light at the bottom. Every one of them filled her with dread, and yet she was pulled down, almost against her will.

Gaia waited for her just off the stairs, and his presence gave her strength.

"Lead the way," she said. The cat looked over its shoulder and then turned and walked across the cellar.

Emma could see the light to her right. It looked like an old oil lamp and flickered, casting shadows and barely chasing away the darkness. The pounding of her heart and the rushing of blood in her ears was almost overwhelming.

Why was she doing this?

A meow in front of her was her only answer.

Gaia walked towards one corner, passing out of the meager light and into the shadows beyond. Emma followed, she could feel a breeze at her back and scooted around, pointing the phone. It cut through some of the gloom but not much, and yet it showed nothing was there. Just the old oil lamp burning in the opposite corner.

Where had it come from? Who had lit it?

Should she go towards it, towards the light or follow the ghost cat into the darkness? Even though logic told her to go to the light, it felt wrong. So, despite her terror, she turned her back and headed after her guide.

Goosebumps rose on her arms. The feeling of dread, the feeling of impending doom was like a weight on her back. It pressed on her chest making each breath tortured. It made her legs heavy and each step difficult. She wanted to run, back to the stairs, out of this house, and to never come back.

A whisper behind her caused her to spin back around. Then it was behind her again, and she spun back. The words were unclear, she could not even discern the intent of the speaker. Was this the one she felt would not hurt her, or the black spirit that wanted her dead?

Gaia came into view of the phone's torch. He was sat next to something, or was he? A blur formed before her and she rubbed her eyes. As she watched, the mist formed into a translucent person. Emma felt the breath catch in her throat, she tried to swallow, tried to speak, but she could not.

The figure was a woman, it was impossible to tell her age, but she didn't think she was old. She wore a white dress and held her arms out to Emma. Though she should have been terrified, Emma felt a sense of calm came over her, and she found herself walking towards the figure. Towards Ursula, for she knew this was her relative, knew she would not hurt her.

Ursula pointed towards the corner. Gaia followed the direction of her arm and walked over towards the corner. There he scratched at the dust floor. Suddenly, Emma understood. They wanted her to find something and maybe when she did, then this would be over.

Emma approached the corner warily. She understood why they had been haunting this place. The atrocities against them were appalling, and she could not understand how anyone could do something so inhuman. Yet, if it was as simple as finding... finding whatever it was, then why had this not ended generations ago?

Did they bring her here to kill her?

She felt something cold touch her hand and looked down. Ursula's insubstantial hand had taken hers and was gently leading her to the corner. The whispering started again, and she could see the figure's lips move, even as she could see the darkness behind it. Yet she could not hear the words. It was just mumbling, and it did not make sense.

Emma slowed down, was she being led to her death?

Chapter Sixteen

The pull of the hand became more insistent as Emma started to slow. She could see that Ursula was becoming anxious. That she wanted her to hurry, but Emma needed to think. What was going on? What should she do?

For a second she froze. Her breath was coming in desperate gasps, and she dropped her head afraid that she would hyperventilate.

"Hurry," Ursula whispered against her ear. "I can't hold them for long."

Emma made a decision. She was here, and somehow she did not think she would get out of this place alive if she argued with this...

woman... spirit... ghost. So, she raised her torch and shone it into the corner. There was nothing there. Just Gaia sat pawing at the soil.

Emma rushed the last few feet before her nerve broke and dropped to her knees. There she began to scrape at the ground. If they wanted to hurt her, they would, but she felt compelled to see what was here. Maybe once she did, this really would be over. Maybe she would survive.

The floor of the cellar was simply dirt, and in this corner, it seemed to be loose, dry, and dusty. She started to dig and almost as soon as she did she found a small bone. It looked like an ulna, the thick forearm bone. It was small... from a child. The feel of it in her hands turned her stomach and yet it made her want to dig more.

She scratched into the ground, desperate now, she scraped, dug, and clawed until she found something else... something...

Letting out a breath she moved the phone to illuminate the object and carefully dig around it. It was a skull, of that she was certain. Tears ran down her face as she tried to free the skull from the ground. It was almost clear when the room dropped 20° in temperature. Mist filled the air as she breathed and she could feel an oppressive presence behind her. It was as if the pressure in the cellar had increased. As if something was crushing her. Before she had the chance to stand, to turn, something hit her hard in the back, and her face was forced into the soil. It felt like knees on her back. As if someone was kneeling on top of her and a hand on her head forced her mouth and nose deep into the loose and dusty earth.

Emma could not breathe, her lungs screamed for air as she tossed, bucked and heaved to try and shake the attacker from her. It was no use, whoever was here was stronger, heavier, and so cold. Where they touched her, even through her clothes, it felt like ice. Involuntarily she took in a breath, and her throat was filled with dust and dirt. Suddenly, she was mortally afraid. This was it, this was the end, and she had failed.

Chapter Seventeen

Emma saw a light before her. It was down a long tunnel, and she reached out to touch it. The aching from her lungs had eased, and she felt as if she was floating. The cold melted away as did the cellar and she felt serene and at peace. Suddenly, she was not alone, but she was not frightened. Turning, she saw Ursula walking towards her. It was immediately obvious that they were related. The same soft brown hair, the same cheekbones, the same full lips. Both had kind eyes though Emma's were brown and Ursula's were a piercing blue.

"I need to talk to you," Ursula said, and she gently took her hand.

Emma felt like she was home, like nothing could hurt her and she nodded.

"We don't have much time," Ursula said. "If you stay too long you will not be able to return."

Emma listened and learned of all the heartache and pain that had stained the house throughout the generations.

Can I be the one to stop it?

"You have to go now," Ursula said. "Thank you for being so brave, and I will help you as much as I can."

The light was gone and replaced with darkness and pain. Emma gasped for breath and then coughed. Her lungs were full of dirt and dust. They burned and ached and yet she was alive. She still felt as if she was floating and she remembered Ursula's words. She started to fight. Flapping her arms and scratching and clawing she grabbed onto short hair and pulled with all her might.

"It's me, Emma, it's me, Brent. You're safe."

Then they were back in the kitchen and the glorious light. Brent rushed straight through to the living room and put her on the sofa. He dropped to his knees next to her and wiped dirt from her face.

"What happened?" he asked.

Emma wanted to explain, but something that Ursula had said to her was nagging at the back of the mind. That there was a presence here that wanted to stop her. She knew about the dark force, the dark spirit that had grabbed her. The one that had pushed her into the ground and tried to smother her in the soil. But what if Brent was helping him? After all, he had taken the other book.

"Emma, why are you looking at me like that?" Brent asked.

Emma started to sob. She had to trust this man for she had no one else and she could not do this alone. "I was researching the house at the library. I was told about a book and that you had taken it. Why?"

Brent rubbed a hand through his short dark hair and sat back on his heels. "It's hard to explain."

He waited, but Emma would not budge, she would have an explanation, or she would make him leave.

"I'm supposed to be a man of logic, right? The detective who finds out the real reason for things. However, I have seen things before that do not make sense. That cannot make sense. I know you have been under stress, but I believed you and decided to check into this house because something did not feel right.

The book tells a tale that is so horrible that I want us to leave this house now and never come back."

"I can't do it," Emma said. "I made a promise... The promise that I would end this."

Brent spent the next half hour trying to persuade her to change her mind. In the end, he realized it would not work, and so, together they read the book and Emma told him what Ursula had said. They told the tale of how Alden Carter had been tricked. How he was afraid of the Bishop and because of that, he tortured Ursula and then pretended that she had confessed. Ursula had been led to believe that her daughter was burned alive and yet, it still did not break her, maybe she knew the truth. For it had not been Ursula's daughter that the Bishop had burned. He could not find her. So, instead, he took a girl about her age, about her size. It was not Ursula's daughter that he had burned alive, it was Alden's. When

Alden found out he hung himself in the exact same spot that he had hung Ursula and he saw to it that his bones and his daughters were left in the house. It became his mission to make sure that none of Ursula's relatives would ever find peace. Over the generations, he drove many of them insane, and at least three had killed themselves in the same spot. Those that hadn't were so bitter that they would not end the constant cycle of pain.

Now it was up to Emma to do so. If she could.

***

"I want to stay, I have to do this, will you help me?" Emma asked.

Brent stood up and turned away from her. For a moment, she thought he would walk out and just leave her there. Instead, he turned back, nodded and offered her his hand. As he did the scent of burning filled the air and the temperature dropped in the house. The lights flickered and died, and they were plunged into darkness. Emma reached for her phone but she had left it in the cellar. Brent pulled a torch from his pocket, and a thin beam of light illuminated the darkness. The scent of burning got worse and the feeling of a presence, a pressure, was undeniable. It seemed to squeeze them until their lungs ached and their chests hurt.

"We have to go, now," Emma said.

Brent took her hand and led her into the hallway. The moonlight was shining through the top window illuminating the hallway. Hanging from a banister were two nooses.

Emma felt her knees go weak, but Brent pulled her forward.

"Wait. I need something from the kitchen."

Quickly, she grabbed the salt and handed it

to Brent. "If you see anything dark, throw this at it. It won't stop it, but it may slow it down. It may give me the time I need."

Brent took the salt while Emma grabbed hands full of the sage, tearing and ripping at it this time and not bothering to use the scissors. She filled her pockets with sage and then grabbed the bell from the window sill. It tinkled in a way that was cold and empty and set her teeth on edge.

It was time.

Emma knew that speed was of the essence and she followed Brent down the stairs with hardly a pause. Waiting at the bottom was Gaia. The cat meowed in an almost friendly way. It was as if he was glad to see them. Then he led them back to the corner.

"Protect me," Emma said to Brent. Then she dropped to her knees and started digging.

One by one she found the bones and piled them at the side. Ursula had told her that she needed both skulls and most of the bones. But it did not matter if she got all as long as she got most of them. So far, she had found many bones, but she could not find the other skull.

Suddenly, the temperature dropped in the cellar, and the smell of burning was overwhelming. Both of them started to cough as smoke clogged their lungs and seared the back of their throats.

"He's here," she said. "You have to stop him while I find the other skull."

As her breath misted before her and the smoke clogged her throat, she could feel the pressure of his presence. Part of her wanted to scream at him to let this go, to let them move on and rest and yet she knew it would do no good. So, she tore at the ground, pulling off a nail as she continued to dig and rake in the dusty soil.

From behind her, she heard Brent grunt and the sound of him hitting the ground. The light flickered, and she was digging in the darkness. Yet she could not stop. Their only hope was that she found the skull.

The sounds of the fight were going on behind her, but she did not have time to look. Suddenly, she felt a cold hand on her shoulder, and she thought it was all over. Yet, when she glanced up, it was Ursula, and she was trying to tell her something.

Emma could not make out the words, could not quite hear her. Then Gaia was back. The cat looked at her, its eyes old and wise, it begged her to follow.

Gaia led her a little way to the right and started clawing at the ground. Emma dug where he had been digging. Then he melted into the air and was gone. Emma gasped but kept digging.

Her fingers hurt, they were bruised and bloody and yet she dug faster and harder until she found something solid.

She had found it, she had found Alden's skull.

Chapter Eighteen

Emma grabbed the skull from the ground, feeling strangely jubilant that she had found it. Everything was coming together, and soon this would all be over. Behind her, she heard a yelp, a dull thud, and then silence.

Spinning around she looked for Brent. He was lying on the dust floor, near to the pile of bones. It felt as if a hand clenched onto her heart.

Was he dead?

Emma did not know, but she heard a whisper in her ear.

"You must hurry."

For a moment she was undecided. Attempt to help Brent or finish this? Next to his still body, the torch pointed at the bones. It left much of the cellar in darkness and lit up the pile like some macabre Halloween decoration.

There was still a faint glow from the oil lamp, but it did little to chase away the shadows this far into the cellar. Emma knew she had to move. That the only way to save Brent was to see this through and so she started to run for the bones.

Behind her, the chains rattled on the wall, and a wail of rage seemed to hit her like a physical force. Not only did she hear the sound but she felt the anger behind it as she was lifted off her feet and sent sprawling across the floor to land near Brent.

She had to hurry, if he was hurt he would need her help.

Emma gripped on tightly to the skull. It

had started to feel slimy and to slide beneath her fingers, as if rotted flesh slithered beneath her touch. She wanted to throw it, to get it out of her hands and to end this quickly. Only that did not seem right.

Gently, she placed the skull on top of the pile of bones.

Stepping over the bones, she touched Brent's shoulder. He was alive, she could feel his body moving as he drew in each breath. A sense of joy passed through her.

"Hurry," the voice was just a hiss, just a whisper, but she understood.

Pulling hands full of sage from her pockets, she spread them all over the bones. Sprinkling them as wide as she could to make sure that all the remains were covered.

A snarl echoed around the cellar and then she felt something hit her. The skin on her arm split beneath her shirt and hot blood soaked into the material. At first, she just felt cold. As if she had been scratched with a lump of ice, but then the pain hit. A scream left her lips, and she felt as if she would faint.

How could she fight this?

The pain spread up her arm and into her shoulder and she could see the darkness forming before her. It was like a bully. One who had to regroup, intimidate, and build up the courage before he could attack. Right now, he was giving her a choice... she could leave, yet she knew it would not last long. Quickly, she looked around, searching for the salt in the shadows. What she saw almost stopped her heart.

There were other shapes, other shadows moving towards her. Emma grabbed the salt and the torch from near Brent. Shoving the torch into the ground so that it splayed out weak light at the specters that surrounded her she backed behind its comforting glow.

Now, what should she do?

For a few moments, she froze. It was as if the whole world had tumbled on top of her and she could not cope with the weight, with the responsibility. At that moment she thought that she had lost her mind and she shut down for a fraction of a second. She gave in.

Gaia was suddenly in front of her and as he brushed past she felt his body. Cold fur pulled over a sawdust-filled sack. It was unreal, and it was enough to bring her back to the cellar. If this... creature... cat... spirit could stand up to the evil before them, then so could she.

Emma tossed salt around the circle and watched as the shapes pulled back. Alden stayed the closest. A wisp of a man, a ghost with teeth bared and bones showing through the smoky filaments that gave him form.

She had to believe he could not hurt her, but the pain in her arm said otherwise.

"Do it now," the words were whispered into her ear."

Where once the feel of the air, the ghost lips on her flesh, would have sickened and frightened her, this time it only gave her courage.

She could do this.

Pulling the bell from her pocket, she tried to remember the words. The incantation that she must perform to banish this stained soul from their realm. All around her the smoky mist coalesced, swirled and seemed to throb with energy. Some of the forms appeared to be fighting Alden, and some appeared to be helping him.

Emma turned away from the raging smoke storm that seemed to bubble and boil before her and rang the bell over the bones. Up and down, right and left she rang the bell, and she shouted, "Ecce crucis signum, fugiant phantasmata cuncta."

Again she rang the bell top to bottom, left to right. "Behold the emblem of the Cross; let all specters flee," this time she said the words in English.

The air seemed to relax, the pressure released just a little and Emma thought that it was working. That she was sending Alden Carter on to another realm. To where she did not know, and right then she did not care. If he were to boil in hell for all eternity then so be it, for he had given her relatives hell for many, many years.

Slowly, she turned to her right. Again she rang the bell, top to bottom. As she raised her hand to complete the shape of the cross, she was hit in the back with such force that it knocked the breath from her lungs. The bell went spinning out of her hands and clattered away across the dusty floor. The torch was knocked over, and the cellar was plunged into darkness.

Emma felt the chill of a body upon her back, and she was forced, face down into the dirt. She could feel the bones poking into her spine, and the hands scratched up her back and across her shoulders as they searched for her head.

Once they found it, she knew she would be forced into the earth once more, and this time she would suffocate. Then this whole cycle would continue. The hatred would endure on and on down the generations until the house collapsed beneath the burden of evil.

Alden laughed in her ear. A blast of cold, fetid air wafted across her. As she tried to breathe, to shake him free, anything to get out from beneath the horror that pinned her down, her hopes began to fade. She had lost. It was over, there was nothing more she could do.

The hand clasped into her hair and pushed her face into the dirt. Screwing her eyes tight and clamping her teeth she tried desperately not to draw a breath. The hand above pushed harder forcing her further into the gritty soil. Her nose, her teeth, her cheeks all hurt as he scraped her face against the coarse stones that she had unearthed.

Emma pushed against him, trying with all her might to lift her face from the ground. Even if just long enough to take a breath for her lungs were burning and her throat longed to draw in sweet, cool air.

Yet she could not lift him, and she could feel herself weakening. Could feel a sense of calm and drifting. The type that came before the end and yet she would not give in. Reaching out with her hands she searched for something to fight with, for anything. Tentatively her fingers touched something, inch by inch she stretched until her hands found a bone and clasped on tight. Though the angle was wrong and she did not have much force, she swung as hard as she could behind her and just for a second the pressure eased.

Emma lifted her hip and rolled the specter from her back. Climbing to her knees, she drew in great lungfuls of air as she scoured the room for the smoky disturbance that was Alden. Left and right she looked back-and-forth, where was he?

Panting, gasping, and trying to regain her breath, she searched among the shadows. Only it was so dark, and there was more she had to search for. On her hands and knees, she scraped her battered fingers across the ground. Looking for the bell, the torch, for anything that could give her an advantage in this situation.

The pressure started to build again and the air filled with smoke. Emma ignored it, it was not real, and it could not hurt her. Her hand clasped onto something cold, and she pulled it out of the ground. A weak light emanated from the torch, and just for a second, she felt relief.

The beam could not cut through the gloom, or the smoky figures that surrounded her. There was a feeling of despair, of animosity rolling off them and all Emma could do was shrink back against the wall and wait for the worst.

Without the bell, she was finished, and soon it would all be over. For a moment, she spared a thought for Gaia and Ursula, where were they? Had even they abandoned her as the hour drew near? As if just thinking about them had drawn them to her she saw Ursula among the surrounding ghosts. She was surrounded, and an argument seemed to be taking place. The smoky figures drifted and formed, coalescing and then dissipating never solid but substantial. It looked like Ursula had problems of her own, she would not be coming to her aid.

"Gaia?" Emma called. "If you can hear me, find the bell, for without it I am lost."

Laughter echoed around the cellar. The soundwaves hit Emma and pushed her backward, and she shrank against the wall. Once more, Alden separated from the smoky figures and appeared before her. There was glee on his face, triumph in his empty eye sockets, for he knew he had won.

Suddenly, Emma was angry, she was not giving in, and she was not going down without fighting. So, she grabbed hold of two of the bones and swung at him. The figure turned to mist and was gone. Emma dropped to her knees and began to search the soil, rubbing her fingers back-and-forth hoping she could find the bell.

A scream was forced from her lips as Alden

stamped onto her fingers and ground down with his heel. Though she tried to pull her hand away, it was pinned, and she was held there completely at his mercy.

Alden raised his arm and, with a look of elation, was about to bring it down onto her head. Emma shuddered and tried to flinch away, but she knew it would be no use.

"Stop this, Daddy." The shape of a young girl appeared before him.

There was something sad about her and yet something strong.

Alden stumbled backward, releasing Emma's hand.

What should she do? It was so dark and yet she scoured the floor for the bell. Until she felt a hand on her shoulder. Emma jerked back and fell onto her bottom. Looking up, she could see the young girl before her. In her tiny hand, she had the bell, and she was offering it to her.

Tears were streaming down Emma's face as she took the bell. This must be Brook, Alden's daughter. This was a child that had been brutally murdered, she had every reason to be angry and to want this violence to perpetuate and yet she was the one who was helping to stop it. "Thank you," Emma whispered.

Quickly she walked back to the bones and started the whole ceremony again. The spirits mumbled as if to try and drown her out. It was like leaves in a storm of the roar of a crowd just too far away for you to pick out the voices.

Ignoring the cacophony, Emma rang the bell, top to bottom, left to right in the shape of the cross while she chanted the words that would banish the spirits. "Ecce crucis signum, fugiant phantasmata cuncta... behold the emblem of the Cross; let all specters flee!" she shouted.

Ursula had told her she needed to do it five times. Once over the bones then to the South, to the West, to the East, and lastly, to the North. After she had completed the second chanting, Alden appeared again. Though his face was hardly there, she could see the fury on it. The temperature in the room dropped, it filled with smoke, and the pressure around them grew to such a point that she felt as if she were being crushed once more. Yet she knew she must not stop. So, she turned again, rang the bell up, rang the bell down, rang the bell to the left, rang the bell to the right. Static was building, she knew something was going to happen and then Alden screamed.

"Let me be," he screamed. "Let me have my revenge."

Little Brook stood in front of her father. As Emma rang the bell and chanted, she could not believe the child would stop him and yet, Brook did not flinch. Everything Alden threw at her she threw back, every time he came at her she held him back, Emma could see that she was weakening. She had two more points to do and then it was over. Part of her felt sorry for Brook, part of her didn't want to banish the child, and yet she knew she must.

The more Brook stopped him, the more furious her father became, and it was obvious that she would lose this battle. All Emma hoped was that she would hold on long enough for her to complete her task.

The air crackled, what little light there was dimmed and Emma was plunged into almost total darkness. She had one more point to do, and she knew she would not make it.

As she raised the bell for the last time the smoky spirits around her separated. Ursula moved to stand next to Brook and so did two more.

Relief flooded through Emma as she rang

the bell for the last time and chanted the words. Suddenly, the pressure dropped, the light from the torch seemed brighter, and the constant hiss of voices mumbling that had filled her head for so long was gone.

Turning around, Emma was surprised to see that the smoky figures were no longer there. She was alone in the cellar with an unconscious Brent.

It was over, and she had won.

Epilogue

Emma dropped to her knees and started sobbing. It was over, she had won, and yet, somehow, she felt bereft. What had happened to Ursula, to Brook? Where had they gone and would they find peace? Behind her, she heard a sound in the dirt. Grabbing hold of the large bone in one hand and the torch in the other she spun around. The bone dropped from her hand. Brent was trying to sit up, so she rushed across to him.

"How are you?" she asked.

He raised a hand to his head and swayed a little bit. "I'm not sure. Are we safe?"

Emma put her arms around him and hugged him tightly. "They are gone, or at least, I think they are. Now, let's get you out of this cellar."

Slowly, she helped him to his feet, across the dusty floor and back up the stairs. The lights in the house seemed suddenly very bright. They were no longer yellow and sickly, and they gave the place a fresh, new feel. As she led him through the kitchen and across the hallway, Emma knew there would be no noose. It just felt different, and she knew that she could find peace here. Guiding Brent to the sofa, she moved the stuffed cat before she laid him down.

"Stay there," she said. "I will get water and a band-aid for your head."

"Any chance of a whiskey?" he asked. "I could really do with something right now."

Emma nodded, she knew just how he felt.

So she returned to the kitchen and prepared a bowl to bathe his head as well as two glasses of wine. It seemed like it was time to celebrate.

***

Brent slept on the couch that night, and the following morning he called in about the skeleton's they had found in the cellar. They were taken away and laid to rest in the local cemetery. Once they were gone, Brent came back to Emma. "How are you?" he asked.

"I'm just fine, now."

"Well, why don't you come and stay at mine for a while? No pressure. Until we find you somewhere else."

Emma laughed. "Why would I leave? This was my family's home, and I know that I can be happy here."

"Then let me throw out that cat and seal up that cellar so it can never be accessed again."

Emma shook her head. "It's just a room, and as for this..." She picked the stuffed cat up off the sofa and put it on a shelf over the radiator. "This was his favorite place."

"Really, you're going to keep it?" Brent's eyes were comically wide.

"Gaia and I did not get on too well at first, but we are friends now. Who knows, one day I may need him."

Brent nodded, and somehow, she knew he understood. As he had said, he had seen things before. Maybe one day he would tell her all about it.

Brent was suddenly looking embarrassed.

"What is it?" she asked.

"I know how much you have been through, with this." He indicated the house. "And before, I know that you don't trust men, but... I was just... well."

"Would you like to buy me dinner?" Emma asked.

A big smile came over Brent's face, and he nodded his affirmative.

There was one thing that Emma had learned over the last few days, and that was that not all people were alike. There were good people, and there were evil, and it would be wrong of her to judge Brent by her experiences with Mark. This house was to be a new beginning, and it looked like it was going to be a good one.

THE END

Never miss a book.

Subscribe to Caroline

Clark's newsletter for

new release announcements

and occasional free content:

http://eepurl.com/cGdNvX

Preview:

The Haunting of Seafield House

30th June 1901
Seafield House.
Barton Flats,
Yorkshire.
England.
01.00 am.

Jenny Thornton sucked in a tortured breath and hunkered down behind the curtains. The coarse material seemed to stick to her face, to cling there as if holding her down. Fighting back the thought and the panic it engendered she crouched even lower and tried to stop the shaking of her knees, to still the panting of her breath. It was imperative that she did not breathe too loudly, that she kept quiet and still. If she was to survive with just a beating, then she knew she must hide. Tonight he was worse than she had ever seen him before. Somehow tonight was different she could feel it in the air.

Footsteps approached on the landing. They were easy to hear through the door and seemed to mock her as they approached. Each step was like a punch to her chest, and she could feel them reverberating through her bruises. Why had she not fled the house?

As if in answer, lightening flashed across the sky and lit up the sparsely furnished room. There was nothing between her and the door. A dresser to her right provided no shelter for an adult yet her eyes were drawn to the door on its front. It did not move but stood slightly ajar. Inside her precious Alice would keep quiet. They had played this game before, and the child knew that she must never come out when daddy was angry. When he was shouting.

Would it be enough to keep her safe? Why had Jenny chosen this room? Before she could think, thunder boomed across the sky and she let out a yelp.

Tears were running down her face, had he heard her? It seemed unlikely that he could hear such a noise over the thunder and yet the footsteps had stopped. *Oh my, he was coming back.* Jenny tried to make herself smaller and to shrink into the thick velvet curtains, but there was nowhere else to go.

If only she had listened to her father if only she had told him about Alice. For a moment all was quiet, she could hear the house creak and settle as the storm raged outside. The fire would have burned low, and soon the house would be cold. This was the least of her problems. Maybe she should leave the room and lead Abe away from their daughter. Maybe it was her best choice. Their best choice.

Lightning flashed across the sky and filled the

room with shadows. Jenny let out a scream for he was already there. A face like an overstuffed turkey loomed out of the darkness, and a hand grabbed onto her dress. Jenny was hauled off her feet and thrown across the room. Her neck hit the top of the dresser, and she slumped to the floor next to the doors. How she wanted to warn Alice to stay quiet, to stay inside but she could not make a sound. There was no pain, no feeling and she knew that she was broken. Something had snapped when she hit the cabinet, and somehow she knew it could never be fixed. That it was over for her. In her mind, she prayed that her daughter would be safe just before a distended hand reached out and grabbed her around the neck. There was no feeling just a strange burning in her lungs. The fact that she did not fight seemed to make him angrier and she was picked up and thrown again.

As she hit the window, she heard the glass shatter, but she did not feel the impact. Did not feel anything. Suddenly the realization hit her and she wanted to scream, to wail out the injustice of it but her mouth would not move. Then he was bending over her.

"Beg for your life woman," Abe Thornton shouted and sprayed her with spittle.

Jenny tried to open her mouth, not to beg for her own life but to beg for that of her daughters. She wanted to ask him to tell others about the child they had always kept a secret. To admit that they had a daughter and maybe to let the child go to her grandparents. Only her mouth would not move, and no sound came from her throat.

She could see the red fury in his eyes, could feel the pressure building up inside of him and yet she could not even blink an eye in defense. This was it, the end and for a moment she welcomed the release. Then she thought of Alice, alone in that cupboard for so long. Now, who would visit her, who would look after her? There was no one, and she knew she could never leave her child.

Abe grabbed her by the front of her dress and lifted her high above his head. The anger was like a living beast inside of him, and he shook her like she was nothing but a rag doll. Then with a scream of rage, he threw her. This time she saw the curtains flick against her face and then there was nothing but air.

The night was dark, rain streamed down, and she fell with it. Alongside it she fell, tumbling down into the darkness. In her mind she wheeled her arms, in her mind she screamed out the injustice, but she never moved, never made a sound.

Instead, she just plummeted toward the earth.

Lightning flashed just before she hit the ground. It lit up the jagged rocks at the base of the house, lit up the fate that awaited her and then it was dark. Jenny was overwhelmed with fear and panic, but there was no time to react, even if she could. Jenny smashed into the rocks with a hard thump and then a squelch, but she did not feel a thing. "Alice I will come back for you," she said in her mind. Then it was dark, it was cold, and there was nothing.

Find out when The Haunting of Seafield house is available **http://eepurl.com/cGdNvX**

About the Author

Caroline Clark is a British author who has always loved the macabre, the spooky, and anything that goes bump in the night.

She was brought up on stories from James Herbert, Shaun Hutson, Darcy Coates, and Ron Ripley. Even at school she was always living in her stories and was often asked to read them out in front of the class, though her teachers did not always appreciate her more sinister tales.

Now she spends her time researching haunted houses or imagining what must go on in them. These tales then get written up and become her books.

Caroline is married and lives in Yorkshire with her husband and their two white boxer dogs. Of course one of them is called, **Spooky.**

You can contact Caroline via her Facebook page:

https://www.facebook.com/CarolineClarkAuthor/

Or via her newsletter: **http://eepurl.com/cGdNvX**

She loves to hear from her readers.

©Copyright 2017 Caroline Clark

License Notes

Printed in Poland
by Amazon Fulfillment
Poland Sp. z o.o., Wrocław